I DID WHAT?

"I still don't understand why a posse would be after any of us," Valle said.

"It's mainly Fargo they were after," Calder told her. "And me, 'cause I was with him. And you, 'cause he helped you out in that little ruckus."

"I haven't done anything to make a posse want me," Fargo said. "You know that."

"I know it," Calder admitted. "You know it, too, and I guess Valle knows it. Don't matter, though. They're after all of us, and you in particular."

Fargo couldn't figure it out, and Calder wasn't helping much.

"Why did they want me?" he said.

" 'Cause you robbed the Ashland bank," Calder said, and he took another sip of his coffee.

THE
TRAILSMAN
#320

OREGON
OUTRAGE

by

Jon Sharpe

A SIGNET BOOK

SIGNET
Published by New American Library, a division of
Penguin Group (USA) Inc., 375 Hudson Street,
New York, New York 10014, USA
Penguin Group (Canada), 90 Eglinton Avenue East, Suite 700, Toronto,
Ontario M4P 2Y3, Canada (a division of Pearson Penguin Canada Inc.)
Penguin Books Ltd., 80 Strand, London WC2R 0RL, England
Penguin Ireland, 25 St. Stephen's Green, Dublin 2,
Ireland (a division of Penguin Books Ltd.)
Penguin Group (Australia), 250 Camberwell Road, Camberwell, Victoria 3124,
Australia (a division of Pearson Australia Group Pty. Ltd.)
Penguin Books India Pvt. Ltd., 11 Community Centre, Panchsheel Park,
New Delhi - 110 017, India
Penguin Group (NZ), 67 Apollo Drive, Rosedale, North Shore 0632,
New Zealand (a division of Pearson New Zealand Ltd.)
Penguin Books (South Africa) (Pty.) Ltd., 24 Sturdee Avenue,
Rosebank, Johannesburg 2196, South Africa

Penguin Books Ltd., Registered Offices:
80 Strand, London WC2R 0RL, England

First published by Signet, an imprint of New American Library,
a division of Penguin Group (USA) Inc.

First Printing, June 2008
10 9 8 7 6 5 4 3 2 1

The first chapter of this book previously appeared in *Louisiana Laydown*,
the three hundred nineteenth volume in this series.

Copyright © Penguin Group (USA) Inc., 2008
All rights reserved

Ⓟ REGISTERED TRADEMARK—MARCA REGISTRADA

Printed in the United States of America

PUBLISHER'S NOTE
This is a work of fiction. Names, characters, places, and incidents either are
the product of the author's imagination or are used fictitiously, and any resem-
blance to actual persons, living or dead, business establishments, events, or
locales is entirely coincidental.
 The publisher does not have any control over and does not assume any
responsibility for author or third-party Web sites or their content.

The Trailsman

Beginnings . . . they bend the tree and they mark the man. Skye Fargo was born when he was eighteen. Terror was his midwife, vengeance his first cry. Killing spawned Skye Fargo, ruthless, cold-blooded murder. Out of the acrid smoke of gunpowder still hanging in the air, he rose, cried out a promise never forgotten.

The Trailsman they began to call him all across the West: searcher, scout, hunter, the man who could see where others only looked, his skills for hire but not his soul, the man who lived each day to the fullest, yet trailed each tomorrow. Skye Fargo, the Trailsman, the seeker who could take the wildness of a land and the wanting of a woman and make them his own.

Oregon, 1860—where Skye Fargo follows a trail of gun smoke and dead men to clear his name.

1

The big man in buckskins leaned against the wall near the closed door of the barn, which smelled of manure, moldy hay, and the tobacco smoke that drifted in thready clouds. The whole place hummed with the talk of the men gathered around the cockpit, a make-shift ring formed by rough boards.

Around half of the pit was a makeshift grandstand to accommodate those who wanted a close look at the fight that was about to begin. Those who hadn't arrived early enough to get a seat had to stand around the other part of the pit, and there was plenty of pushing and shoving for position.

Skye Fargo's lake blue eyes watched as the men jostled one another and crowded closer to the ring. Some of them were well dressed, a banker or two, and maybe a lawyer. Others wore rough work clothes that hadn't been washed in a while. According to Dodge Calder, Fargo's friend, one of them was the town marshal.

Fargo didn't look like any of them. His fringed buckskins seemed a little out of place, and it was clear that he was accustomed to being outside in the open, not closed up in a building like the bankers.

Only a couple of women were present, both of them soiled doves from some local saloon, Fargo figured. Their faces were avid with anticipation, and it was likely that they'd make a good bit of money from the customers who'd be eager for their favors later, after their blood had been stirred by the fight to the death between two roosters.

Money changed hands and bets went down. Fargo heard an occasional nervous laugh, indicating that some of the bettors were a little unsure they'd made the right choice.

On one side of the ring a man with a corncob pipe clamped between his teeth watched as another man took the hood off the orange-colored head of a fighting cock with its comb and wattles trimmed so that its opponent in the coming battle couldn't grab them with its bill.

The man with the pipe removed it from his mouth and breathed a cloud of smoke into the cock's face to agitate it, not that it didn't appear agitated enough already.

Both men wore ragged shirts and denim pants that showed hard use. Lank hair hung down from their sweat-stained hats.

On the other side of the pit, the handler of the opposing cock spoke soothingly to it and almost seemed to cuddle it as he checked on the short, sharp metal spurs affixed to its legs where its own spurs would have been. Fargo couldn't make out the handler's eyes because they were hidden by a hat pulled down low on the forehead so that the features were obscured.

"That kid's been braggin' about how many fights that big black bird's won," Dodge Calder said. He took off a battered hat and ran skinny fingers through his thick white whiskers. "You might wanna make a bet on that cock. Name's Satan."

The kid's rooster was so black that it was almost purple. It stretched its long neck toward its handler as if listening carefully to what was being said. Its wattles and comb had been trimmed like the other bird's.

2

"I don't bet on things I don't know much about," Fargo told Calder.

Calder nodded. "Don't blame you. The Bryson brothers don't lose often."

Fargo had known Calder for a long time, and in fact he'd stopped off in Ashland to see him after leading some pilgrims up the Applegate Trail to the Willamette Valley. Calder had been a guide for a few years, which is how Fargo had gotten to know him, but Calder had liked Oregon so much that one year he'd decided to stay and see if there was any gold left in the area that some of the forty-niners had drifted to when the pickings got slim in California.

As far as the Trailsman knew, Calder hadn't found any gold, but he'd found himself a home in Ashland, a little farther to the south of the gold fields. He'd done some trading and trapping and was making a living for himself one way and another.

Fargo was happy for Calder, but he wasn't interested in settling down in one spot, no matter how easy it might be to make a living there. He was a natural wanderer, not cut out to be tied to one place for any length of time.

There wasn't a lot to do in Ashland, and Calder had suggested the cockfight as a bit of entertainment on a Sunday afternoon. Fargo didn't see much amusement in a couple of roosters trying to kill each other, but Calder wanted to get a bet down.

"I got my money on the Brysons," he told Fargo. "The kid's been lucky, but those old boys have been at this a long time, and they don't like to lose. That rooster of theirs is rough as a cob. They call him General Washington, and he's won four fights in a row. Fact is, nobody around here will fight against him. That's why we got such a good crowd. Folks wouldn't turn out like this to see just an ordinary fight."

Satan against General Washington, Fargo thought.

3

If the birds lived up to their names it would be quite a fight.

Fargo was about to say something along those lines to Calder, but someone moved a board aside and the referee stepped into the ring. He was the man Fargo thought might have been a lawyer. He walked to the middle of the ring and took a thick watch out of the pocket of his black frock coat. The crowd grew quiet.

"One round of thirty minutes is what we've agreed on, gentlemen," the referee said. "Is that correct?"

The Bryson brothers, who didn't look like any gentlemen Fargo had ever seen before, nodded.

"Or 'til our rooster kills that one," one of the brothers said.

The other brother grinned. The kid ignored them.

"Very well," the referee said. He backed up a little. "Bill your birds."

When he said that, one of the Brysons nodded to his brother and stepped out of the ring.

"That's Hap," Calder said. "He's the cheerful one."

Hap didn't look cheerful to Fargo. He looked mean as a cornered cougar.

"The other one's Willie," Calder said.

Willie looked just like Hap to Fargo. As far as he could tell, they might have been twins.

Willie took General Washington to the middle of the ring, holding the cock's legs together with its body draped over his left arm. The kid walked up to him, holding Satan the same way. They let the two birds glare at each other, keeping them a foot or so apart. The birds squirmed for a couple of seconds as if trying to escape, but their handlers gripped them tightly. When the gamecocks saw they couldn't get free, they started to stretch their necks and peck at each other, trying to reach an eye or some other soft spot. Their handlers pulled them back before they could make any contact.

The sparring went on for a short time, maybe half

a minute. Fargo didn't see much point to it. The birds already hated each other plenty. They didn't need any encouragement.

"That's enough," the referee said. "Get ready."

The handlers backed away from the center of the ring and squatted down with eight or nine feet of empty space between them.

"Pit your birds!" the referee called out, and as he did the handlers released the cocks. The quiet exploded in a flurry of feathers. The spectators pressed around the ring. They yelled, shoved each other, and made more bets.

What happened between the cocks was almost too fast for Fargo to follow. The kid's bird flapped its clipped wings and seemed to go straight into the air as if on a spring, and then to descend on General Washington before the cock had a chance to gain any height. After that, the birds attacked each other, heads darting, feet scrambling, spurs flashing.

Fargo thought that if he'd been more used to cockfights, he'd have been able to follow what was happening better, but because he didn't know what to watch for, the subtleties, if any, were lost on him.

General Washington, however, was getting the worst of it. Fargo could see that much. Satan was pecking furiously at the general's head from his superior position, trying to get at the eyes, but the general was strong and somehow got out from under his opponent and scuttled away to the side. The kid's rooster backed away a short distance, the clipped tips of his outstretched wings quivering.

The two birds glared at each other for a couple of seconds like human fighters might as each took his opponent's measure. Then they rushed forward and launched themselves into the air.

This time General Washington got off to a good start, as did Satan, and the birds smacked together a couple of feet above the ground, their wings working

5

rapidly. Their feet kicked so fast that they were just a blur, but neither bird could land a solid blow with either spurs or beak.

Before they fell to the ground, Satan pulled out a couple of the general's feathers, and a few drops of blood hit the dirt of the barn floor as the feathers floated down.

The crowd got rowdier. Most of the men were yelling encouragement at one bird or the other and slapping each other on the back. Even Calder, a man Fargo didn't consider excitable, jumped up and down as he strained to see over the heads of the men in front of him.

The birds rushed together again. Fargo thought they must have been tiring because they didn't gain much altitude. The pecking was just as furious as before, though, and Satan ripped out quite a few more of the general's feathers.

Fargo glanced at the Brysons. They stood stiffly at the side of the ring, stony silent, arms crossed, eyes narrowed. The kid, on the other hand, sat leaning against the boards, to all appearances as calm and relaxed as if sitting in church with a clean conscience.

The fighting cocks clashed again, this time without rising from the ground. Satan got his beak into General Washington's neck and twisted. The birds fell to the ground, and Satan flapped his wings to rise above the general. He hacked at the general with his spurs, slashing at his eyes.

The general's neck writhed as the bird tried to avoid the stabbing spurs, but one of them sank into his left eye. The general jerked his head away. Blood spurted, and the general went into a frenzied backward dance, his legs hardly touching the ground as he spun and flipped. He fell on his back in the dirt, his wildly beating wings stirring up a small gray storm.

Then he stopped and was still. Satan walked over

to the dead bird and hopped onto the body. He looked around the ring slowly and crowed.

Hap Bryson jumped into the ring, his face twisted with rage. Before anyone could stop him, he reached the birds and gave Satan a vicious kick, sending him flying from General Washington's body.

The referee ran toward Bryson. "Stop it, Hap! Get out of the ring!"

Hap either didn't hear him or didn't give a damn. His hand reached for the pistol at his side, and he jerked the gun from its holster.

The kid jumped up and ran toward Hap, but he was too late. The revolver in Hap's hand roared. Satan exploded in a bloody mass of feathers.

The kid landed on Hap's back, fingers tearing wildly at his eyes. Fargo thought for a second that Hap might meet the same fate as General Washington.

Willie Bryson must have thought the same thing because he leaped to his brother's aid. He had a wide-bladed knife in his hand. He crossed the pit with a couple of long strides, and raised the knife to strike at the kid's back.

At that point things started to go to hell.

The boards surrounding the ring collapsed as men pushed forward. The kid and Hap fell and disappeared from view in the roaring, trampling crowd. Fargo couldn't tell if Willie had stuck the kid with his knife. He could no longer see Willie, either, as the brawl engulfed them.

"Well, damn it," Calder said. "We just gonna stand here, or are we gonna do something?"

It wasn't Fargo's fight, but he hated to see the kid killed by a couple of bad losers.

"Let's go," he said, and he and Calder waded into the crowd, which was already beginning to break up into smaller fights, the participants having forgotten what had started things in the first place and being interested only in protecting themselves or their money. Or maybe just in fighting for its own sake, as a flattened nose or a mashed lip seemed to make everybody purely happy.

The money had some effect, though. In the first moments of the melee, a good bit of it had been scattered around on the ground, and some of the men were snatching it up, while others were trying to take it from them.

Fargo heard a cracking noise and looked past the fighting just in time to see the grandstand collapse. Men toppled to all sides, though some of them didn't even stop fighting, clinging to their opponents as they hit the ground.

Fargo returned his attention to the brawl in front of him.

One man sat on another, his hand on the back of the man's head, rubbing his face into the dirt. Two others stood upright as they pounded each other with their fists. Some kicked those who were down, and others knocked down those who were up. One man who was bent double to pick up a coin got kicked upright and then fell on his face when someone hit him in the back of the head.

Fargo ducked and dodged, trying to get to the kid. He avoided a flying fist, kicked a man in the groin, and pulled another man away from a pile where he thought the kid had gone under.

A snarling man grabbed Fargo's arm.

"What the hell you think you're doin'?" he said, drawing back his hamlike fist while keeping a firm grip on Fargo.

Fargo didn't have to answer or bother to defend himself, as Calder was behind the man. Calder hooked his arm around the man's neck and yanked him backward.

Calder was skinny but wiry. He tightened his arm and the man's face, already red with rage, became even redder because he could no longer breathe. He clawed at Calder's arm and kicked backward with his booted feet, but Calder just grinned and hung on.

Fargo turned back to the mob. He glimpsed a leg sticking out from under a couple of men. Reaching down and grabbing hold, he dragged the kid from under an unconscious form and past the feet of a couple of fighters. The kid's shirt was torn, and blood ran down one arm. Willie must have made a little slice, Fargo thought, but not enough to kill anybody. He didn't see Willie anywhere.

The kid tried to stand up but was too shaky. Fargo put out a steadying hand, but the support wasn't enough. The kid started to fall. He was a skinny one, and Fargo swept him up in his arms.

Fargo turned to find Calder, who was still clinging to his larger opponent, though they'd fallen to the ground, where they were both in danger of getting their heads kicked or stomped.

"You can let him go now," Fargo said, kicking the man in the head. Calder rolled the bigger man off him and got to his feet.

"We better get our asses out of here before somebody notices us and takes a notion to stop us."

Calder was pulling open the barn door when Willie Bryson came tearing out of the uproar and caught up with them. He struck downward with his knife, narrowly missing Fargo, who had heard him just in time.

Fargo turned and, without dropping the kid, kicked Willie in the knee. The knee bent the wrong way. There was a popping sound, and Willie collapsed with a thin cry. He dropped his knife, curled into a ball, and wrapped both hands around his knee.

"Let's get outta here," Calder said, and Fargo carried the kid outside into the sunlight.

Calder pulled the door closed. "What now?"

"You got us into this," Fargo said. "You think of something. Where did this kid come from?"

"I don't know. Just showed up here yesterday, got friendly with some of the bigwigs and asked about getting up a cockfight. The Brysons were happy to oblige him."

The Brysons didn't look happy now, and Fargo was pretty sure they'd never looked like bigwigs.

"I didn't mean the Brysons are very much around here," Calder said when Fargo asked him. "You saw some of those men in there. The referee's Jim Thomas, owns the bank here. Judge Rascoe was in there, too."

He might have said more, but Fargo interrupted him. "I don't care who was there. We need to get rid of this kid."

"We sure do," Calder said, looking over Fargo's shoulder.

Fargo turned his head and saw the barn doors opening. The first man through the gap was Hap Bryson. His pistol dangled in his hand.

"Too bad somebody didn't flatten him," Calder said.

Hap raised the pistol and fired a shot. The bullet buzzed over Fargo's head.

"Horses," Calder said, running around the side of the barn to a small corral. Buggies and wagons were parked around the corral, and several horses, including Fargo's magnificent black-and-white Ovaro stallion and Calder's bay, were inside.

Calder jerked open the gate.

"Hold the kid," Fargo said, and handed his burden to Calder.

He swung up onto the big Ovaro, reached down, and took the limp form from Calder, laying it across his lap. Calder grabbed the reins of his bay and held it while he flapped his hat and shooed the other horses out of the corral.

"Might as well confuse ever'body we can," he said, before climbing into the saddle.

Hap and those following him were met by running

horses. Calder and Fargo went in the opposite direction, scattering clods of dirt behind them.

Fargo looked down at the kid and wondered what he'd gotten himself into. A few minutes ago, he'd been watching a cockfight. Now he was galloping away with someone he didn't know with no destination in mind. He noticed for the first time a dark bruise on the side of the kid's head.

He noticed something else, too. The kid's features were soft and feminine, and the freckled cheeks had never been shaved.

"I'll be damned," he said.

"I expect you will," Calder said. "What for this time?"

"This kid," Fargo said. "He's a woman."

"Can't be a 'he' if it's a woman."

"You know what I mean."

"I guess I do. You right sure about what you're sayin'?" Calder paused. "Hell, yes, you are. If there's a woman within a mile, you'd know it. What're we gonna do with her?"

"She's still unconscious," Fargo said.

He didn't know what had hit her, but she showed no sign of waking up. She had been able to pass for a young man because she was slim and small breasted, but she'd had to keep her hat pulled low because nobody getting a really good look at her face with its upturned, freckled nose and its bow of a mouth would have made a mistake about her sex. Fargo admitted to himself that after a good look at her, he couldn't think of her as a kid anymore.

Fargo pulled on the reins and slowed the Ovaro. Calder did the same with his own horse and they rode side by side for a few minutes without talking. They'd left any semblance of a trail behind them and rode through a forest of towering fir and pine trees. Fargo didn't know where they were, but that didn't bother him. If there was a trail around, he'd find it. For that matter, he didn't really need a trail.

He was a little worried about the woman, however. Her arm had stopped bleeding. The wound wasn't much more than a scratch. But the bruise bothered him.

"Well," Calder said after a while, "I guess they didn't come after us. That ain't like the Bryson boys. They believe in gettin' even."

"For what?" Fargo said. "Nobody did anything to them."

"The kid there did. Her rooster killed theirs, and that's enough for them."

"You telling me they never lost before?"

"Not with some bird that jumped on theirs and crowed about it. That must've made 'em madder'n hell. Sure stirred things up, too."

"And left us stuck with the kid here. The woman. What do we do with her?"

"Maybe she's dead," Calder said, but even as he spoke the woman finally stirred on Fargo's lap.

Something in Fargo stirred, too. You put a woman that close to him, and it was only natural that he'd respond, even if it was a woman dressed in a man's clothing.

The woman lay still for a minute or so. Then she turned her head and looked up at Fargo.

"Who are you?" she said.

Her voice was deep and husky, another thing that had helped her pass for a man, Fargo thought.

"Name's Fargo," he said. "That's Dodge Calder there on the other horse. You got a name?"

"Valle. V-A-L-L-E. But pronounced like 'valley.' "

"That's all? Just Valle?"

"Valle Wilson. I feel strange."

"You got a right to," Calder said. "You got hit in the head. Pretty hard, too, to judge by that bruise you got."

Fargo stopped the Ovaro and helped Valle down. She was a little steadier on her feet than she'd been in the barn but not by much. Fargo let her have a drink from his canteen, and she stood for a while after drinking, bracing herself on the side of the big stallion.

"I'm better now," she said.

She loosened the tie that held her hat and removed it, revealing thick blond locks. She ran her hand through them, shook her head, and replaced the hat.

"You sure you're all right?" Fargo said.

He admired the fair hair, having a weakness for blondes. Or for just about any good-looking woman when you came right down to it.

"Pretty sure," Valle said.

She put up her hand. Fargo gripped it and pulled her onto the Ovaro's back behind him. She leaned into Fargo, and he felt the pressure of her small, firm breasts against his back.

"What happened?" she said.

"Your rooster won the fight," Calder said. "Remember that?"

"I remember. Then that man shot Satan."

"And you jumped him," Fargo said. "Sorry about your rooster."

"It wasn't about the rooster. I have other roosters. It's just that a man who'd do that kind of thing ought to be shot himself."

She was quiet for a minute, then went on. "I guess I should thank you. I don't remember much of anything after I jumped on that man's back, but you must have gotten me out of a bad fix back there."

"You're sure welcome," Calder said. "What we were wonderin' is what we're gonna do with you."

"Do with me?"

"We can't take you back to Ashland," Calder said. "The Brysons would get you. Besides, other folks might not like you so much after all that ruckus."

"Some of them lost their money in the fighting," Fargo said. "They won't be getting it back."

"None of that's my fault."

"Folks might not see it that way," Calder told her. "Best you go on back home. Where might that be?"

"Up around Roseburg."

"Used to be called Deer Creek," Calder said, as if Fargo didn't know. "You're a long way from home, Valle."

"Not so far."

"You come down here just to take our money with that rooster of yours?"

"That's right. I needed money, and I knew there were some fights around here my birds could win."

She didn't sound entirely convincing to Fargo. He said, "You must have put a pretty good bet on the one you called Satan."

"I did. I knew he'd win."

Again, Fargo wasn't convinced. He hadn't seen her make any bets. Of course, she might have made them before he and Calder arrived at the barn.

"That money's gone," Calder said. "Won't be a sign of it left in that barn. People were grabbin' for it with both hands."

"I know the money's gone," Valle said. "But I have to go back there. I can't go home to Roseburg without my horse and wagon. They're at the barn. A couple of my other roosters, too."

Fargo hadn't thought about how she might have arrived at the barn. The idea of going back didn't appeal much to him.

"No way around it," Calder said without waiting to hear what Fargo thought. "We gotta take you back."

"Beats taking her to Roseburg, I guess," Fargo said after a second.

He turned the Ovaro's head in the direction they'd come from. Taking Valle back would relieve him of any further responsibility, which was a good thing, because the whole situation bothered him. Something wasn't quite right about Valle's reactions and statements, though he couldn't figure out exactly what it was.

"You know how to get back to the barn, Fargo?" Calder said.

"I know."

Calder laughed. "I was just teasin' him, Valle. They call Fargo the Trailsman. He can follow any trail there is, and he can find a trail where there ain't one. He ain't never been lost in his life."

"I'm glad to hear it," Valle said, but she didn't sound glad. She didn't sound impressed, either.

She had nothing else to say on the way back to the barn, though Calder kept up a one-sided conversation for a few minutes. Finally he gave up. Fargo didn't mind, and Valle didn't seem to notice.

When they neared the barn, Calder said, "I'll just go on a little ahead and see what's what."

"Good idea," Fargo said, reining in the Ovaro.

Calder rode off, and Fargo sat patiently, very much aware of the woman behind him. If she was aware of him, however, she didn't mention it. She didn't say anything at all. Fargo wondered what she was thinking about.

After ten minutes or so Calder rode back. "Looks all right to me. Sam Taylor owns the place, and he's a friend of mine. The wagon's still there, and Sam says nobody's been back to look for us. Ever'body lost interest after we cleared out, I reckon."

Fargo hoped he was right. He flicked the reins, and the Ovaro moved forward.

The wagon sat in back of the barn not far from the corral. Sam Taylor, a bandy-legged man with a black beard, stood by the wagon smoking a cigarette.

Valle raised up and looked over Fargo's shoulder.

"Where are my roosters and cages?" she said, deepening her voice. "They were in the back of the wagon."

Taylor took his cigarette from his mouth, tossed it down, and ground it out with the toe of his boot.

"Sorry to have to tell you this, kid," he said, looking up at Valle and Fargo. "The Bryson boys broke the cages and killed the roosters. I was able to keep 'em from doing any damage to the wagon."

Valle slid down off the Ovaro's back. "I thank you for that." She went to the wagon and looked over the sideboards at the remnants of the smashed wooden cages. "Where are the roosters?"

"I took 'em off," Taylor said.

He didn't offer any further explanation, but Valle appeared to be satisfied. Fargo figured the man would be having fried chicken for supper.

"I thank you, Mr. Fargo, and you, too, Mr. Calder," Valle said. She climbed up on the wagon seat. "And you, Mr. Taylor. Now I'd better be going."

Fargo thought she was taking things too calmly, as if she was in a bigger hurry to get away than she should have been. If it had been his roosters that the Brysons had killed, he'd want to have a word with the two men. Maybe Valle didn't think there was much she could do about it, and she was probably right, but she should have been more concerned.

The old mule hitched to the wagon didn't look like he could make a very long trip, but Fargo knew that mules often looked like that and still managed to travel a few hundred miles. Anyway, it wasn't Fargo's worry, any more than any of the rest of it had been. If Valle wanted to go on home, he was happy to let her, though he had to admit that he wouldn't have minded getting better acquainted with her. He imagined he could still feel the heat from the slim body that had pressed up against him as they rode.

Valle flicked the reins and kicked off the wagon's brake. The old mule started to move, but it hadn't gotten far before Fargo heard shouting in the distance. He turned to see who was making the noise.

It was the Bryson brothers. They were riding hard. And they weren't alone.

2

The shooting started even before the riders got within range, but the bullets came close enough to bother Fargo. He didn't know what was going on, but he didn't plan to stick around and find out. Whatever it was, he didn't think he'd like it.

"What the hell?" Calder said.

"Damned if I know," Taylor said, and he took off for his barn at a bandy-legged run.

Fargo dug his heels into the Ovaro, and as he passed the wagon seat, he reached out for Valle. She didn't hesitate. She took his arm and pulled herself astraddle the big stallion as it ran for the trees. Dodge Calder was close behind them.

Once inside the cover of the towering trees, Fargo slowed the Ovaro and looked back. No one was in sight, and he hoped that Taylor had been able to stall the mob—if they hadn't burned down his barn and killed him.

"What was that all about?" Fargo said.

"Looked like a posse," Calder told him. "It was the Bryson boys in the lead, but the town marshal was with 'em. So was his deputy."

"Why were they shooting at us?" Valle said. "What have you done?"

"We ain't done a thing," Calder said. "I'm thinkin' you were the one they was after."

"I didn't do anything. They killed my roosters."

"One of the Brysons did. There was a lot more than Brysons in that bunch. Like I say, it looked like a posse."

"You can go back later and find out," Fargo said. "Right now we'd better put some distance between us and them. You know these woods?"

"Nobody knows these woods," Calder said. "Not much, anyway. Mighty easy to get lost in here. For anybody except you, I mean."

"Then let's lose them," Fargo said.

A couple of hours later Fargo figured the riders had either gotten lost or given up. He hadn't seen or heard them since leaving Taylor's place. For that matter, Valle and Calder seemed pretty confused themselves about where they were. It was getting late in the afternoon, and the sun was slanting through the trees, brightening the green boughs.

Fargo stopped in a clearing made by a lightning strike. A big fir had been split down the middle and then fallen over, taking down some smaller trees as well. That had been a while back, and the fallen branches had all turned brown.

"We'll stop here," Fargo said. "We can spend the night if we have to. Dodge, you might want to go back to Taylor's place and see if he can tell you why that bunch was after us."

"I don't know if I can find my way," Calder said, shaking his head.

"It's not far," the Trailsman told him. "We've been riding in a big circle, mostly. I'll show you the way."

He threw his leg over the Ovaro's neck and slid to the ground. Valle looked down at him.

"You don't think they'll find us?"

"If they do, it'll just be blind luck. I figure they're tired of looking and headed home for supper."

"You don't know the Bryson boys like I do," Calder said. "Or the marshal, neither."

19

"And I sure don't want to meet them. I've got some beans and jerky and coffee. We can have something to eat before you go to Taylor's. When you come back, bring Valle's wagon with you."

"Might as well go now," Calder said. "I don't want to be wanderin' around in these woods after dark. If I get to Taylor's place before night, I can find my way back, I guess. You say you can tell me how to get there?"

Fargo told him. Calder wasn't sure about it, so Fargo scraped some dead pine needles out of the way and scratched a rough map on the ground.

"Think you can find it now?" he asked.

"I hope so. What're you gonna do while I'm gone?"

"Wait for you," Fargo said. "Have some coffee and grub, maybe."

"Fire might bring the Bryson boys."

"I don't think so. You're the one who needs to be careful. They could be waiting for you when you get back."

"I'll be careful. You don't have to worry about that. If the Brysons or the marshal's there, I'm not gonna show myself. I hope they didn't do nothin' to Sam."

"It was us they were after."

Calder nodded. "Sure looked that way."

He turned his horse's head and rode off in the direction that Fargo had showed him. In a couple of seconds he had disappeared into the trees.

Fargo turned his attention to Valle, who still sat astride the Ovaro.

"You planning to sit there all day?" he said.

She slid off the horse and stood looking at Fargo. She was shorter than he'd thought. The top of her head didn't come up to his chin.

"Why do you think those men were after you?" she said.

Fargo was getting a little tired of questions like that, and it showed on his face.

"I don't have any idea. They don't even know me. I've never spent any time around here before. Maybe that means it wasn't me they were after."

Valle looked puzzled. "You mean they were after your friend?"

Fargo couldn't be sure, but he thought she was only pretending to be baffled.

"I don't think so. Dodge has lived around here for quite a while, and they wouldn't have any reason to turn on him now."

Valle took off her hat and shook out her hair. "You can't possibly think they were after me."

The note of surprise was just about perfect, but Fargo didn't believe it was real. He eyed her slim figure, well concealed in the loose-fitting pants and shirt. Her blond hair hung down halfway to her shoulders. She was pretty, and she was smart. And he was convinced that she was a liar. Either that, or she was holding something back.

"They were after you, all right," he said. "Had to be. I couldn't tell you why, though. Maybe *you* can tell *me*."

She put her hands on her hips. "No, I can't. I haven't been here much longer than you have. All I did was set up a cockfight. They wouldn't be shooting at me for that."

The last part of what she said was true, and it made Fargo wonder all the more just exactly what was going on. She wasn't going to tell him, not now, so he'd just have to bide his time until she decided to talk.

"How about some coffee?" he said.

Valle looked around the clearing. "No, thanks." She walked to where the big tree had fallen. Its trunk had lost some of its boughs, but there was a sheltered spot that seemed to attract her. She dropped down to the ground. "I think I'll just sit here and rest."

Fargo joined her, leaving the Ovaro to crop the thin grass nearby. The Trailsman sat cross-legged beside her and said, "How did you get started in cockfighting?"

Valle looked off into the trees, but as far as the Trailsman could tell there was nothing to see. It was just about twilight, and he heard an owl hoot off in the dimness.

"It was my daddy who got me started," Valle said. "He raises the roosters at our place and sells them. He takes them to fights, too, sometimes. I helped him now and then, and I decided I liked it."

"I never saw the point of it," Fargo said.

Valle shrugged inside her loose clothing. "Some people don't. Others do. President Washington had fighting cocks."

"The rooster I saw today?"

Valle smiled at him for the first time. When she did the corners of her eyes crinkled.

"No, not the rooster. That was *General* Washington. He was named after the president, though, I guess."

Fargo wasn't much interested in Washington, either as president or general. He said, "Why didn't your father come here with you?"

Valle turned her gaze away from him, back to the trees. "He had other things to do."

Fargo didn't believe it, any more than he'd believed most of the other things she'd told him, but he let it go. They sat in silence for a few minutes, and then she turned to him.

"Did you ever feel lonesome?" she said. "I don't mean the kind of lonesome you get on a Sunday afternoon sometimes. I mean the deep-down kind of lonesome that hollows out your stomach and makes you want to cry. Do you even know what I mean?"

Fargo could have said a lot of things. He could have told her how he'd lost his whole family when he was just a kid and how it felt to be suddenly alone in the world with nobody to depend on but yourself. Somehow, though, he got the feeling that she already knew that. So all he said was, "Yeah. I know."

"What can you do to make the feeling stop?"

"I'm not sure it ever does. After a while it kind of fades, but it never goes away."

She turned to him and clutched him. "I want it to go away."

He wondered why the lonesome feeling had settled on her, and he started to say that he couldn't make it go away, but she didn't give him a chance. She pressed herself to him and kissed him fiercely.

Fargo was so surprised that at first he didn't react the way he normally would have. His instincts took over soon enough, however, and he returned the kiss. Her mouth was hot, and his tongue found hers. She wrapped her arms around him, and they slid down onto dry fir needles.

Eventually Valle broke the kiss. She sat up and started undoing her shirt buttons. She whipped off the shirt and flung it aside, revealing her lithe body. Fargo had thought her breasts were small, and they were, but they were perfectly shaped, with dark nipples that jutted out hard and proud.

Fargo reached up and covered her breasts with his hands, and she arched her back to force them against his palms. The nipples seemed hot as fiery brands. She threw her head back, her mouth open, as Fargo caressed her breasts, making slow circles with his palms as the nipples grew even harder.

Valle uttered a short cry and jumped up, shucking off her pants in seconds. Fargo marveled at the tangle of blond curls at the juncture of her thighs, and then he was up and getting out of his own clothing, which suddenly seemed to be constricting his breathing.

When he was naked, he pulled her to him. She pressed against him, trapping his rock-hard shaft like a burning log between them.

Fargo started to kiss her, but she pulled away and dropped to her knees, taking his powerful pole in both hands and moving them slowly up and down it, giving special attention to the sensitive tip. After a few seconds of that, she held him with one hand while she licked the shaft, starting low and sliding her tongue all the way to the end. Then she took the end in her mouth, using her lips and tongue to rouse him to even greater excitement. He thought he might explode at any moment, but she stopped and said, "Not yet."

She lay back on the fir needles and drew him down to her.

"Your turn," she said. "I hope that beard of yours won't scratch me."

Fargo would have told her that he'd never had any complaints, but he didn't trust himself to speak. He lowered himself to her and slipped his head between her legs. She locked them behind his neck as he began to tease her with his tongue, first using it to slide along the lips and nudge aside the blond curls, then moving it inside them to the little button that would give her the most pleasure.

When his tongue touched the right spot, she moaned deep in her throat and then said, "I want you in me now, Fargo. Please. Now!"

Fargo lifted himself and sought her with his erect shaft. It parted the lips of her sex and slipped inside easily. Fargo had planned to begin slowly, but Valle was having none of that. She thrust against him with frantic urgency, her movements stimulating his own, and almost immediately they were moving in an unrestrained fever of passion.

Valle reached her peak quickly and gave a series of short, sharp cries. Fargo hadn't quite achieved completion, so he remained within her while he caught his breath. It didn't take him long, and it didn't take Valle long, either. She began to rotate her hips beneath him, and within moments they were again riding the fury of their desire without any consideration of time or circumstance.

For a fraction of a second the thought passed through Fargo's mind that if Dodge Calder were to come back early, it would be a mite embarrassing, but the thought passed, and Fargo couldn't have done anything to stop what was happening to him even if Calder showed up with the Bryson brothers and the entire posse. Valle moaned and thrust against him as his juices burst out of him like lava, thick and hot. She clasped him to her and shook while her own culmination shuddered through her slender frame.

When it was over and they were calm, they dressed and sat waiting for Calder.

"I've never felt quite like that before," Valle said. "You're quite a man, Fargo."

Fargo didn't ask her if she felt any less lonely. It was possible that she did, but the feeling wouldn't last long. He thought she might talk some more and tell him more about what she was doing in Ashland or clarify some of the other things he wondered about, but she seemed to prefer silence and didn't offer any further explanations.

It was another hour or so before Calder returned, and by then it was dark in the woods. Looking up through the trees, Fargo could see the stars blinking in the black night sky. The moon was big, full, and white, and it cast thick shadows among the trees around the clearing.

Fargo heard the rattle of the wagon long before he saw Calder coming, so he wasn't worried. He figured that anybody sneaking around in the woods wouldn't be making as much noise as Calder was.

When Calder finally emerged into the clearing, Fargo saw that he was riding in the wagon, his horse tied behind.

"I don't see no fire," Calder said when he climbed down off the wagon seat.

"We decided not to have any coffee," Fargo said.

Calder looked at him in the moonlight. "What'd you have, then?"

"Never you mind," Valle said, standing beside Fargo. "Thank you for bringing the wagon. Now I can go home."

"Not through these woods," Calder said. "It was hard enough to get that thing this far. You couldn't make any kind of long trip in it. You'll have to find a road."

"Dodge and I will make sure you get home all right," Fargo said.

"Not so sure that'd be a good idea," Calder said.

"Why not?" the Trailsman asked.

" 'Cause we might be better off stayin' out of sight for a while."

The night breeze sighed through the firs. Calder didn't say anything more.

"You planning on telling me why?" Fargo said.

" 'Cause of what I heard from Sam."

Calder looked down at his feet and kicked away a dead twig.

"You want to tell me what that was?" Fargo said. Getting any real information out of the old pelican was like pulling teeth.

"Well," Calder said, leaning back against the wagon, "it's kind of a complicated story. I could sure use some of that coffee you were gonna boil, except you didn't. There's a little barrel of water there in the wagon in case you need any."

Fargo knew he wasn't going to get any more out of Calder at the moment, so he got the coffeepot while Calder started a small fire. Soon enough the Arbuckle's was boiled and ready. Fargo poured the first cup for Calder, careful not to get any of the grounds in it.

Calder took a sip of the scalding liquid, not seeming to notice how hot it was, then smacked his lips.

"Mighty good," he said. "Sure wish we had some beans and biscuits to go with it."

"I can fix something," Valle said.

"Not until he tells us what he found out," Fargo said. "Go ahead, Dodge. Start talking."

After one more sip of coffee, Calder said, "Here's the way it was. When I got back, the Bryson boys and their friends were gone. Sam wasn't too happy to see me, and he wanted to get me off his place and gone as fast as he could."

He drank more coffee while Fargo thought about what he'd said. Which wasn't much, Fargo decided.

"What was the marshal doing with the Brysons?" he asked.

"Seems like the marshal was leading that bunch, not the Brysons. It was a posse, like I thought."

"But I still don't understand why a posse would be after any of us," Valle said.

"It's mainly Fargo they were after," Calder told her. "And me, 'cause I was with him. And you, 'cause he helped you out in that little ruckus."

"I haven't done anything to make a posse want me," Fargo said. "You know that."

"I know it," Calder admitted. "You know it, too, and I guess Valle knows it. Don't matter, though. They're after all of us, and you in particular."

Fargo couldn't figure it out, and Calder wasn't helping much.

"Why did they want me?" he said.

" 'Cause you robbed the Ashland bank," Calder said, and he took another sip of coffee.

3

The story that Fargo finally got out of Calder didn't make any sense at all, but Calder swore it was the truth.

"Sam's the one did the tellin'," Calder said, "and he didn't have any reason to lie about it."

The truth, according to Sam Taylor, was that while the cockfight was going on in the barn, the bank in town was being robbed.

"It was that same gang that's pulled off a couple of jobs around this part of the state," Calder said. "You might've heard about 'em."

Fargo hadn't, but Valle had.

"Nobody knows who the leader is," she said. "They always come into town and get away easily. Not a single one of them has ever been caught or wounded or anything."

"Seems like they've been mighty lucky," Fargo said.

Calder nodded his agreement. "They sure enough have. Lucky enough to make a fella wonder."

"Wonder what?" Valle said.

"Wonder if somebody's not helpin' 'em out," Calder said. "Gettin' some inside information that'd make their job easier for 'em."

"Why single me out as the leader?" Fargo asked.

" 'Cause you're new in town. Been hangin' around with a known good-for-nothin' named Dodge Calder, who might be lookin' to make a little easy money by settin' up a bank robbery."

"People here know you better than that," Fargo said. He paused. "Don't they?"

"Most of 'em do. Have to say that some who know me don't like me a whole lot."

"You're talking about the Bryson brothers," Fargo said.

"Yeah, I am. They never liked me, and they sure as hell don't like you, not with the way you got Valle away from 'em. The way Sam told it, they're the ones who convinced the marshal you're behind the robbery."

"How did I set it up?"

"With me helpin' you. I introduced you to a few folks in town. You might've talked to 'em about the bank."

Valle put her hand on Fargo's arm. "You could go to town and tell them that you didn't have anything to do with the robbery. The people you talked to would back you up."

"The Bryson brothers would like it if Fargo went back," Calder said. "He wouldn't get a chance to get anybody to back him up. The Brysons'd shoot him off his horse before he said a word."

"So you think they're watching for me?" Fargo said.

"Damn right they are. The posse wasn't gonna waste any time searchin' these woods. Too easy for 'em to get lost. They might even be hopin' that *you* got lost. But if you show up back in town, they'll be ready for you. 'Specially the Brysons."

The situation didn't sound promising to Fargo. He hadn't intended to make enemies of the Brysons, but it appeared that he had.

"What does the marshal think of all this?" he said.

"He's a first cousin to the Brysons. What does that tell you he might be thinkin'?"

"That he'd believe his cousins before he'd believe

a stranger. I guess I won't be going back with you, Dodge."

"Back with me? You think I'm goin' back? I can't do that, not 'til that gang stops their robbin' or gets put out of business. The Brysons have told folks I'm a part of it. They'd as soon shoot me as you. Maybe they'd like it better, since they've known me longer."

"What about your friend Sam?"

"He's not sure what to think. On the one hand, he's known me for a long time. On the other, there's a posse out lookin' for me. He was good enough to let me take the wagon and leave, but what he's askin' himself is, why would a posse be lookin' for me if I wasn't guilty?"

"But neither one of you was anywhere near the bank," Valle said.

"Don't matter none to the Brysons. They say we were just gettin' ourselves seen so nobody would think we was in on the robbery."

"We weren't too smart, were we?" Fargo said. "Considering the way things turned out."

"Nope. Our clever plan didn't work. The Brysons were too smart for us and figgered it all out."

Fargo thought it over. He didn't like the idea of being on the run from the law, but from what Calder said, going back to try to straighten things out wasn't going to work. It might be better for him to just move along, even though turning away from trouble went against the grain for him. Sooner or later the law would catch up with the bank robbers, but until that happened, Fargo would stay out of this part of the country. If Calder wanted to go along with him, that was all right, too.

He couldn't leave quite yet, though. He felt an obligation to see that Valle got home safely.

"Well, I guess we can do that," Calder said when Fargo told them his intentions. "Just as long as we don't let too many people know where we are."

"I don't plan for anybody to know," Fargo said. "We won't be telling the Bryson brothers. At least I won't."

"Me neither, but what if the Bryson brothers come lookin' for us there?"

"They don't know who I am," Valle said. "They think I'm a young man. They wouldn't be able to find me."

"What about the marshal?" Fargo asked Calder.

"He can't find his butt with both hands. Long as we're gone, he won't look too hard for us. Wasn't nobody killed, so that makes him even less likely to keep after us. The bank will push him, so he might scout around town for a while, but that's all he'll do. He wouldn't want to tangle with the whole gang. Not even the Brysons'd want to do that."

Valle said, "Even if all that's true, I don't need your help getting home. I've already caused you enough trouble."

Fargo insisted. "If you run into somebody who's looking for me and Dodge, you might get treated rough. Better if we're along with you in case of trouble."

Valle tried to talk him out of it. It was almost as if she was more afraid of what might happen to her if he accompanied her than if she went alone. Fargo wouldn't listen. Neither would Calder.

"Fargo's right. If the Brysons have put out the word about us, they'd be sure to mention you. You might as well let us tag along, just to be sure you get home all right. Where did you say you lived?"

"Close to Roseburg." Valle gestured vaguely. "Out from there a ways."

"Not in town?"

"No. Not in town."

Calder looked at Fargo. "Nobody's going to be looking for us there. Valle's right about that. Maybe we could stay at her place for a while. Kind of lie low while we wait for the Brysons and the marshal to forget about us."

"What would your father think about that?" Fargo asked Valle.

Valle didn't answer for a while. She seemed lost in her thoughts.

"Well?" Calder said, a little impatiently.

"I don't know if he's there. He travels some. With the roosters."

"We wouldn't be any trouble to you," Calder said. "We could help out around the place."

Valle's shoulders slumped as she gave in. "All right. You can stay if my father agrees."

"What if he's not there?"

Valle didn't meet his gaze. "We'll just have to see."

"You ain't got a mama?"

"She died," Valle said. Fargo was about to say that he was sorry, but she added, "It was a long time ago. I was too little even to know about it."

"I guess that's settled, then," Calder said. "We gonna leave now, or wait 'til tomorrow?"

"No use in starting out in the dark," Fargo said. "We'll leave at first light."

"Fine with me," Calder said. "Now how about those beans? I could sure use some beans and biscuits about now."

"I'll see what I can do," Fargo told him.

Fargo and Calder slept on the ground that night, with Calder's snores reverberating across the clearing. Valle slept in the wagon. Fargo thought about joining her, but he didn't think Calder would appreciate it. Though with all the snoring he likely wouldn't have heard a thing.

The next morning, Calder insisted on coffee before they got started, and then they had to decide what to do about the wagon. It was either leave it there or look for a path through the forest, a path that they all knew didn't exist.

"I like to not made it back here in that thing," Calder said. "Too much brush in the way, too many limbs hangin' down. No way but to leave it."

He held his tin cup upside down and banged on the side of the wagon to get the last of the coffee out before stashing the cup away.

"Wouldn't hurt you to ride the mule," he said to Valle. "We can leave the wagon here, cover it up with some of these dead limbs. It'll keep 'til this mess is cleared up, and then you can come back for it."

Valle shook her head to show she didn't think much of that idea, but she saw the wisdom of it and agreed without putting up much of an argument.

"Too bad we ain't got a spare saddle," Calder said after the decision had been made.

"A real gentleman would give up his saddle for a lady," Fargo said with a grin.

"I'm an old man," Calder protested, touching his white whiskers. "Got a lot of aches and pains from sleepin' on the ground last night. Wouldn't do for me to have to sit the spine of this bony old horse of mine."

"That horse looks pretty well fed to me," Fargo said.

"That's all you know about it. You're a youngster and better padded than I am around the bottom. You oughta give up your saddle if anybody does."

While they were talking, Valle got a couple of old saddle blankets out of the back of the wagon and spread them on the mule's back. The mule turned to look at her with its long ears cocked at an angle.

"There's a rope in the wagon," Valle said after the blankets were in place. "If one of you *gentlemen* can make me a hackamore for Sara here, we can get started."

"Sara?" Calder said. "What kind of a name is that for a mule?"

"A good one," Valle said. "I've ridden Sara before, but I didn't expect to have to on this trip. I had the blankets along just in case. I had a bridle, too, but it's missing. Your friend Sam must have taken it, him or the Brysons, when they killed my roosters."

"Sam wouldn't take it. You say you got some rope?"

"Right here," Valle said, reaching into the wagon for it. She tossed it to Calder. "Think you can fix something up with that?"

"Quicker than a minnow can swim a dipper," Calder said.

He took the rope and had a hackamore on the mule in a couple of minutes. The mule didn't seem pleased with the proceedings but didn't balk. When he was satisfied with his rigging, Calder led the mule over beside the wagon, where Valle sat on the seat.

"Ready to go," he said.

Valle stepped off the seat and onto the mule's back. She took the improvised rein from Calder and said, "Let's get out of here, then."

"Me and Fargo gotta cover up the wagon," Calder said.

"Don't worry about it," Valle told him. "Who's going to find it here? And if somebody found it, how would they get it back to town?"

"It'd be hard for 'em," Calder agreed, "but some folks will do anything to steal something like a wagon."

"If somebody wants it that much, let it go. I can always get another wagon."

Valle touched her heels to the mule's sides, and it ambled forward.

Calder looked at Fargo, who just shrugged and nudged the Ovaro to follow. Calder went along after them, looking back over his shoulder at the clearing and the wagon that sat there empty and solitary.

It took them most of two days to get to Roseburg. They kept to the woods for the most part, and while the going wasn't hard, it wasn't easy, either. Fargo got tired of pushing pine branches away from his face.

It seemed to him that the closer they got to Valle's home, the quieter she became. She hadn't smiled much since he'd known her, but now she didn't smile at all. She didn't seem to want to talk about whatever was bothering her, so Fargo didn't press her for conversation.

They avoided the town of Roseburg and rode to a small spread a mile or so out of town. It was well off the road, and no other houses were near.

"You must like your privacy," Calder said as they approached the house, a small cabin that appeared to have maybe three or four rooms.

"People and noise bother the roosters," Valle said. "And the roosters bother the people."

Fargo figured she was right about that. There must have been twenty roosters in a large pen near the house. Lord knows what kind of racket they'd raise around sunrise.

The pen was well shaded by firs, and the roosters were all tethered to stakes near small shelters. Fargo knew it wouldn't do to let fighting cocks mingle freely together. Before long, you wouldn't have very many of them left, if you had even one.

There was a small barn in back of the house, and beside it was another chicken pen, but this one was different from the other. It contained just some hens scratching and pecking in the dirt. Breeding stock for the fighting roosters, Fargo supposed.

A horse was tied to a hitch rail in front of the house. A young man came out of the door and watched them as they reined to a stop.

"Hello, Valle," he said, but he was taking a suspicious look at Fargo and Calder when he spoke.

"Hello, Tom," Valle said. "Have you been taking care of things?"

He was young, around Valle's age. He had a smooth

face and clear blue eyes. A shock of black hair showed under his hat. He wore a pistol high on his hip.

"I fed the roosters this morning and gave them fresh water," he said. "Where's your wagon?"

His real question was, *Who are these men?* Valle answered both the spoken and unspoken questions.

"I had to leave the wagon back in Ashland. It has a broken axle, and I didn't want to wait for it to be fixed. These two fellas were kind enough to see me home. Skye Fargo and Dodge Calder."

"Pleased to meet you," Tom said, but Fargo could tell by his tone that he wasn't pleased at all.

Fargo supposed that Tom helped out when Valle's father was on the road with the roosters, but he sounded like more than just some hired hand.

"Tom lives around here," Valle said, as if that would clear everything up. "He helps out when nobody's around."

"Yeah, I'm a big help on the place. I take care of everything that needs doing."

He looked at Fargo when he spoke, as if making sure that Fargo got the idea.

"Mr. Fargo and Mr. Calder will be staying around for a day or two," Valle said, and Tom's look darkened. "Then they'll be moving on."

If she thought the last statement would brighten Tom's appearance, she was wrong.

"We don't need any help," Tom said. He continued to stare balefully at Fargo and Calder. Mostly at Fargo.

Valle either didn't notice his tone and his stare or pretended she didn't. She got off the mule. "I'm going inside. I'm sure Mr. Fargo and Mr. Calder could use something to eat. It's been a long trip, and I'm tired."

Fargo liked the way she kept calling him and Calder *Mister*. It made him feel almost like he was a member of civilized society, which he wasn't and never would be. He could pass for it when the occasion demanded, however, and maybe this one did. There were undercurrents to the talk that he didn't understand.

Fargo climbed off the Ovaro and tied the reins to the hitching post. When he stepped up onto the little porch of the cabin, Tom nudged him with his shoulder, pushing him a couple of inches to the side.

Fargo didn't take offense. He knew what jealousy could do to a man, even when there was no real basis for it. Tom had all the marks of a jealous man, and in this case there was some basis for the feeling, though Tom couldn't have been sure of that.

"You need to watch where you're going, Fargo," Tom said.

Calder was right behind Fargo. "You're the one needs to watch, son. Fargo didn't do any shovin'. You did."

"Who asked you, you old coot? Don't you know better than to butt in when somebody else is talking?"

"Wasn't buttin' in. Just statin' a fact."

"Bullshit," Tom said, and gave Calder a shove that sent him stumbling off the porch and into the yard, where he sat down so hard that his hat came off.

Calder jumped up, grabbed his hat, and swatted it against his hip to get the dust off.

"You sorry little turd, pushin' an old man around. You come down here, and I'll teach you a lesson."

"I don't have to come down there, old man. I can teach you one from right here."

Tom's hand reached for his pistol, but it never got there. Fargo caught his wrist and stopped his draw. Tom turned to him, his face red with anger.

"Let go of my arm."

"You need to calm down some before I do," the Trailsman said.

Tom kicked him in the shin and jerked his wrist free. Before he could draw his pistol, Fargo threw a short, hard punch into his belly. Tom staggered off the porch and into the yard, where Calder hit him with his hat.

"Teach you to mess with me, by God," Calder said, whipping the hat back and forth across Tom's face. "Call me an old coot, will you?"

Tom took hold of Calder's shirt and threw him down. He reached for his pistol again, and this time he got it out of the holster.

"Hold it," Fargo called to him.

Tom spun around and fired. The bullet chipped splinters off one of the rough posts that held up the roof of the porch and slammed into the wall of the house.

Fargo's big Colt barked once and Tom went down to his knees, a look of surprise on his face. He dropped his pistol as if it had suddenly become too heavy to hold and fell forward on his face.

Calder walked over to the fallen man and toed him with his boot.

"Looks like you killed him," he said.

He didn't sound sorry about it, and Fargo couldn't find a whole lot of regret in himself, either.

"Didn't have time to do anything else. He was going to shoot you, and he tried to kill me. What got into him?" Fargo looked back into the house. Valle was nowhere to be seen. "Was he crazy?"

"Acted like it. You see Valle in there?"

Fargo shook his head and slid the Colt back into its holster.

"Where'd she go?" Calder said.

"I don't know, but I think we better find her."

It took only a minute to discover that Valle wasn't in the little house.

"Back door's wide-open," Calder pointed out. "She went in through the front and never even stopped. Probably never slowed down. Went straight on through and out the back. I wish I knew what the hell was goin' on around here."

38

Fargo would have liked to know, too. He'd just killed a man who'd seemed intent on killing both him and Calder, and Valle had disappeared without a word. Those two things, added to the way Valle had acted ever since they'd saved her at the barn in Ashland, had Fargo wondering.

"What're we gonna do about that fella in the front yard?" Calder said. "Can't just leave him there. Reckon we oughta let somebody know what happened?"

"The law?" Fargo said.

"Well, now, that might not be a good idea. That marshal down in Ashland might have put out the word on us dangerous bank robbers, even if he's too lazy to look for us himself. Wouldn't do us much good if we went into town with a dead man laid across his saddle, even if he hasn't."

Fargo nodded his agreement.

"Guess we could bury him," Calder said, " 'fore he starts smellin' bad. And somebody's bound to come around askin' questions, sooner or later. Just as well if there ain't no bodies lyin' around."

"We're not going to be here later," Fargo said.

"Where we gonna be?"

"I don't know yet."

"You thinkin' we oughta look for Valle? She can't be too far off. Mule's still right here."

"She could be hiding anywhere," Fargo said. "She knows the area, and we don't. No use to look for her."

"Sure. So you got a plan?"

"We'll bury Tom. I didn't know him long, and I didn't like him a bit. But it's not right to leave him lying there."

"That's the truth. We better see to the horses first and bury him after we do. And then what?"

"We'll see if there's anything to eat around here," Fargo said.

"Oughta be plenty of eggs," Calder said. "I like mine scrambled. What about after we eat?"

"After that, well, we'll have to figure something out."

"I'll look around for a shovel," Calder said.

By the time they got Tom buried it was just about dark. Calder went inside to rustle up some eggs, and Fargo walked over to the big pen to take a look at the roosters. Most of them looked a lot like Satan, but there were a couple of white ones, and a few were a slate gray color.

He stood outside the pen and watched them for a few minutes. They didn't seem bothered by his presence. They went about getting ready for sleep as if he weren't even there. He figured they were hostile mainly to other fighting cocks.

It wasn't long before Calder called him back inside. Fargo could smell coffee by the time he got to the porch.

Calder had a fire going in the woodstove in the little kitchen, and a big iron skillet sat on top of it beside a coffeepot.

"You like your eggs runny or stiff?" Calder asked. "I like 'em about middleways between, myself."

"That'll be fine," Fargo said.

"Won't be any trouble to do yours a little different."

"Middleways is fine."

Calder finished the eggs and scraped them from the pan onto a couple of plates he'd set on the table. He poured coffee into two chipped cups, and they sat down to eat.

"Couldn't find anything else," Calder said. "Had to gather the eggs myself. Looked like nobody'd seen to 'em lately. That Tom wasn't much of a hand around the place if you ask me."

Calder was right, and Fargo wondered just what Tom had been. If Valle had been there, she might have told them. Or, considering how secretive she'd been up until that point, she might not.

After they'd eaten and cleaned up the kitchen, Fargo and Calder went out and sat on the porch. Fargo rolled himself a cigarette, and Calder did the same. The night air was cool, and the stars glittered above the tops of the fir trees in the distance.

"Be fall before long," Calder said. "Wonder how them chickens get through the winter."

Fargo mentioned the shelters.

"Yeah," Calder said. "I guess they'd do it." He took a last drag off his cigarette and tossed it away. It bounced on the ground in a little shower of sparks. "You come up with a plan yet?"

"Not yet," Fargo said. "We'll stay here tonight, then see what we can think of in the morning."

"Be an early morning with all them roosters crowin'."

Getting up early had never bothered Fargo, and he didn't think it would bother Calder, either.

"You gonna sleep inside?" Calder asked. "There's a couple of beds. I think I'll give one of 'em a try."

Fargo didn't have any objection to sleeping under a roof and in a bed now and then, as long as it didn't turn into a permanent thing.

"Which one you want?" Fargo said.

"The one belongs to Valle's daddy. I wouldn't feel right sleeping in a woman's bed."

"I don't think it'll bother me," Fargo said.

Calder grinned. "I'll bet it won't."

Fargo judged it was a little after midnight when he heard the noise outside. It wasn't the chickens that had awakened him but someone trying to move stealthily across the front yard.

The Trailsman lay in the bed and waited. His pistol was already in his hand when he heard the first tentative step on the porch. By the time the door opened, he thought he knew who the intruder was, and he put his pistol down on the floor beside the bed. Best to have it handy in case he was mistaken.

41

There was no door on the little bedroom, and when the opening was darkened by a slight form, Fargo was sure he'd been right.

"Good evening, Valle," he said.

Valle flinched but didn't speak until she was inside the room near the bed.

"Is that you, Skye?" she whispered.

"It's me. Were you thinking it might be Tom?"

"I wasn't sure. Even when I heard the snoring from Daddy's room, I wasn't sure."

"Hard not to recognize that snore. You must've thought Tom was going to get rid of us for you."

"I didn't know what to think. You don't know what he's like. You don't know what *they* are like."

Fargo sat up on the edge of the bed and reached until he found his makin's in the pocket of his buckskin shirt that hung from a nail on the wall. He rolled a cigarette and lit it with a lucifer he snapped into life with his thumbnail. In the brief flare of light, he saw what might have been fear in Valle's eyes.

"You might as well tell me about it," he said.

Valle looked around the dark room as if worried that someone else might be there. "Where's Tom?"

The tip of Fargo's cigarette glowed as he drew the smoke into his lungs.

"Tom's not around right now." Fargo breathed out smoke. "You don't have to worry about Tom."

"You don't know how it is."

"Maybe not, but I know you don't have to worry about Tom. He's beyond all that kind of thing now."

"What do you mean?"

"I mean he's dead."

Valle sighed and sat on the floor by the bed. "I'm not sorry to hear it."

"Tell me about him."

"I'm afraid to tell."

"Maybe you didn't understand. There's no reason to be afraid of Tom anymore."

"It's not just Tom. It's all of them."

Fargo pinched the coal at the end of what was left of his cigarette and the small spark disappeared. The only light in the room was moonlight through a small window high on the wall.

"Who's *them*?" he said.

"The bank robbers," Valle said. "Tom was one of them. He was here to be sure I didn't mess up."

Now they were getting to it, but what she said just made Fargo more confused.

"How are you connected to the bank robbers?" he said.

"I'm the distraction they used for the robberies. At least I was in Ashland."

"Most of the men in town were at the cockfight," Fargo said, getting the idea now. "The bank robbers didn't have to worry much about anybody coming after them."

"That's right. They got the posse together after everything was over and done, and then they had you to blame."

"They couldn't have planned on that part."

"No. But the rest of it was all figured out in advance. If Satan won the fight, I was supposed to strut around and cause trouble, get a ruckus started somehow. It worked out better than I thought, thanks to the Brysons."

The gang couldn't have counted on the Brysons being so upset, Fargo thought. He said, "They were lucky. Why didn't you just go to the law?"

"That's the part that makes me afraid. They have my father. They said they'd kill him if I didn't cooperate."

Fargo thought that over. "Well, you cooperated. Are they going to let him go?"

They listened to the snoring from Calder's room for a minute or so before Valle answered.

"No," she said. "They're not going to let him go. That's why I came back."

Now that she'd started telling her story, Valle went ahead and told it all. The robbers had been successful a couple of times, but they hadn't tackled a bank as big as the one in Ashland. It had some large deposits because of the sawmill there, and they wanted to be sure things went smoothly. So they decided they needed a diversion.

"I don't know why they settled on us," Valle said. "I guess they'd heard of my father or seen some of the fights he's put on. They came here, and they took him."

"Just took him?" Fargo said.

"We couldn't fight them. There were too many of them, and they all had guns. They came riding up, the whole gang of them, and there was nothing we could do. They'd have killed us both if we'd argued. They told us what they were going to do, and Pa went with them. They left Tom to watch me."

Fargo had been seriously wrong about Tom, who hadn't been jealous at all. He'd been suspicious.

"Tom was here," Fargo said. "You were in Ashland. He wasn't watching you there."

"Someone was. They told me that someone in the crowd would be one of their men. So I had to do as I was told, or they'd kill my father. I have one more job to do, and they'll let him go then, or so they say."

"What's the job?"

"I have to go to Jacksonville and stage another fight. I have one week to set it up. It has to be on Saturday afternoon at two o'clock."

"And you had to come back for another rooster."

"Three or four. I can't go with just one."

"Tell me about the bank robbers."

Valle took a deep breath. "The one in charge is called Wolf. I don't know of any other name for him.

He has a beard. Not like yours. His face is covered with hair so you can hardly see his eyes. He even looks like a wolf. There were others with him when he came here, but they didn't give any names. I heard one of them called Big Boy. He's tall and fat. Taller than you, even. He tried to talk Wolf into letting him stay here instead of Tom." Valle shuddered. "But Wolf just laughed at him."

"You don't know where they took your father?"

"No. I don't have any idea. They have a place somewhere, but so far nobody's been able to find it."

"What do you do now?" Fargo said.

"I came back hoping that you might have chased Tom off. I was so afraid that something terrible would happen, I just left. I heard the gunshots, but I kept right on going. I know you must think I'm a coward."

Fargo didn't think that. He just figured she was looking out for herself. If Tom had been in the bed when she came back, she'd probably be talking to him now, telling him how Fargo had forced her to bring him back.

But he was the one who'd been tricked. He suspected she'd hoped all along that he and Calder might get rid of Tom for her. That was why she'd finally given in and allowed them to come with her.

"Will you help me, Skye?" she said.

He wanted to say that he would, but for some reason he held back.

"I'll think about it. We'll talk it over with Dodge in the morning."

Valle put a hand on his leg. "That's my bed you're sleeping in, you know."

"I kind of figured it was."

"I think there's room in it for both of us, though."

Fargo grinned in the darkness.

"We could give it a try."

"What if your friend hears us?"

"The way he's snoring, he couldn't hear it thunder."

"We'll find out," Valle said, and in a flash she was out of her clothes and in the narrow bed with him.

Their mouths met in a kiss that rapidly grew more heated and urgent. His hand cupped her left breast and his thumb found the hardening nipple.

Valle's hands clutched at his shoulders as her arousal heightened. Fargo released her lips and lowered his head to her breasts so that he could suck first one nipple and then the other between his lips. His tongue circled them teasingly. Valle arched her back as if urging him to take more of the firm, creamy globes into his mouth. As he continued his oral caresses on her breasts, he reached down and insinuated a hand between her thighs, rubbing her mound. Valle grew wetter under his touch.

Valle said huskily, "Your turn," and put her hands on his shoulders to move him back a little on the small cot. That gave her room to return the favor he had done for her. She gently sucked his nipples in turn, all the while running her fingers through the thick mat of hair on his broad chest. Fargo responded with a deep groan of sheer pleasure.

After subjecting him to several minutes of exquisite torture, Valle began kissing her way down his lean, well-muscled body. She ran a hand over his groin and felt the hardness waiting for her there. Valle took hold of the shaft with one hand and squeezed it affectionately. Fargo groaned again.

Valle lowered her head still farther and began to plant kisses around the head of his organ. Then she pressed her lips against it up and down its length. The thick pole of male flesh throbbed in her hand as she began to lick it. Finally, she parted her lips and took the crown into her mouth, sucking on it with an urgency that was intense yet tender.

Fargo's strong hands caught at her hips, maneuvering them toward his head. He reached up with his hands, found the heated wetness at her core, and used his thumbs to spread open the folds of her sex. He lifted his head, his tongue flicking several times against the sensitive nubbin at the front of her opening. As Valle cried out in ecstasy, Fargo speared his tongue into her. She responded by sucking harder on him and cupping his balls in her hand.

Both of them spiraled higher and higher until Fargo sensed that they were nearing the point of no return. As much as he enjoyed what they were doing, he wanted more. With a passionate gasp he began trying to shift around again. With seeming reluctance, Valle let him go. That reluctance vanished quickly as she took a new position poised above his hips. She reached down to grasp his shaft and guide it into her as she sank down on him, impaling herself on the iron-hard spike of his manhood.

When he was fully sheathed within her, she began rocking her hips back and forth, occasionally throwing in a circular rotation that made them both moan. As she rode him, he stroked her thighs, her belly, and her breasts. Valle leaned forward, and Fargo cupped her face and brought it to his so that he could press his lips gently to hers.

That gentle kiss soon grew rougher and more demanding on the part of both of them. His tongue circled hers in a sensuous duel that made their passion roar higher. Valle's hips bounced harder, making Fargo's member slide slickly in and out of her at an even faster pace. He thrust hard into her, giving her the pleasure she demanded from him. Her fingers dug into his shoulders as she gripped him hard and rode him as if racing for her life on a galloping bronco.

Fargo felt his climax boiling up, and as Valle began to spasm again on top of him, he knew there was no need to hold back. He grabbed her hips and pulled her down hard against his shaft. She threw her head back, closed her eyes, and panted softly as Fargo began to gush inside her, emptying himself in throbbing culmination.

With every muscle in her body going limp, Valle fell forward on him like a puppet with its strings cut. Fargo wrapped his arms around her, cradling her as Valle gave a deep, heartfelt sigh of satisfaction.

Yep, Fargo thought, there had been plenty of room for both of them in the bed.

4

Fargo was up early the next morning, ahead of Calder, but not before the cocks. Someone had once told Fargo that chickens could see daylight a full half hour before a man could, and Fargo believed it. The morning still seemed totally dark to him, but outside the house there was enough noise on the place to raise the dead from their graves. Fargo thought he might better go check on Tom, make sure he was still where he'd been planted, but he didn't figure it was worth the trouble.

Instead he went outside to the pump and washed up. The splash of cold water on his face was a shock, and it took his mind off the crowing. By the time he got back in the house, Valle already had breakfast cooking on the stove.

Eggs again. Fargo thought he might turn into a chicken if he had to stay around this place very long. Then he remembered what Valle had said last night. One week until the bank robbery in Jacksonville. It would take them a couple of days to get there, and a couple of days to set up the fight. That meant they wouldn't be around here long enough for him to start sprouting feathers. At least he hoped not.

Along with the eggs, Valle also cooked up some biscuits, which Calder hadn't done the previous evening, and made coffee. It wasn't a bad meal, but Fargo liked a little more variety.

Calder didn't seem to mind. He dug in with gusto.

"Glad to see you back, Valle," he said with his mouth full of eggs and biscuit. "You sleep all right?"

He cut his eyes at Fargo when he said it, but the Trailsman didn't acknowledge the glance.

"Just fine," Valle said. "There's nothing like sleeping in your own bed."

"Guess that means Fargo'll be sleepin' on the floor for a while," Calder said. "I got dibs on that other bed already."

Fargo didn't mind the subtle kidding. He nodded and said, "I'm used to sleeping on something hard."

Calder laughed. "I'll bet you are, Fargo. I'll bet you are." He ate some more. "Those roosters do make a hellacious noise, don't they? I guess you're used to gettin' up early, Valle."

"That's right. It's good that I do, because the morning is when I work with the cocks."

Calder cut his eyes at Fargo again, but the Trailsman looked straight ahead.

"I'll be mighty interested to see how you do that," Calder said.

Valle just gave him a little smile, and Calder gave up. They finished breakfast, and while Valle was cleaning up, Fargo and Calder drank coffee. As they did Fargo explained the situation.

"Let's see if I got all this straight," Calder said, setting his empty cup on the table. "We're gonna help somebody named Wolf rob the bank up in Jacksonville so he'll let Valle's pa go. You really believe he'll do that?"

Fargo glanced back at Valle, who seemed to be paying no attention to them.

"I'm not sure if he'll do it. He says he will."

"I guess he got the name 'Wolf' because of his kind

and gentle ways. Always helpin' out people who don't have as much as he does and suchlike."

Fargo had been thinking along the same lines. Why should Wolf let Valle's father go when he could kill him a lot easier? And not have any witnesses left around who could tell where he'd been hiding out, either.

"We might have to do more than let them rob the bank," Fargo said.

"Like what?"

"Catch them. Get Valle's father back for her and prove that I didn't help rob the bank in Ashland at the same time."

Calder laughed. "You and me? An old man and a Trailsman? I know you're tougher than a grizzly bear, but you're just one man. You think we could go up against Wolf and his gang that nobody can catch, whip 'em, and save Valle's pa?"

Fargo grinned at him. "I didn't say it'd be easy."

"You sure as hell didn't. It won't be, neither. That Jacksonville bank's likely to be a rich one, and Wolf ain't gonna just roll over and let you rub his tummy like some old tame town dog."

"Why would the bank be such a rich one?" Fargo said.

" 'Cause that's gold-minin' country. More'n one old boy's made himself a pile up that way, and a good bit of that money's in the bank there."

Fargo had known about the mining, but it hadn't occurred to him in connection with the robberies. It was as if Wolf was working up to make his biggest strike his final one.

"You got some kind of a plan?" Calder asked.

"Not yet. I thought we'd just go on to Jacksonville and see what we can do."

"Sounds like a hell of a mess to me," Calder said with a shake of his head.

It sounded that way to Fargo, too. But the more Fargo thought about it, the less he liked being blamed for a bank robbery. That kind of thing could follow a man around, cling to him like a burr. If he could prove that Wolf was the leader of the gang, then he'd be in the clear.

Besides, Fargo had never been the sort of man to ride away from trouble. He'd always gone at it head-on, and devil take the hindmost.

"Time for me to exercise the cocks," Valle said from behind him. "Do you really want to watch, Dodge?"

Calder jumped to his feet. "I sure enough do. That ought to be a sight to see."

Fargo thought so, too. He stood up and said, "Lead the way."

Valle went outside, with Fargo and Calder following close behind. She went to the pen for the cocks, and for the first time Fargo noticed that there was another narrow pen that ran along the side of the one that enclosed the cocks.

"That's the run," Valle said, pointing it out. "That's where I'll exercise the cocks."

"All of 'em?" Calder said as he looked out over the big pen full of roosters. "That'll take you a while."

"Only the ones I'll be taking to Jacksonville. I can't exercise all of them every day."

"Which ones will you be taking?" Calder said.

"The best ones."

"Which ones would those be?"

"Those four," Valle said. She pointed to the four cocks nearest to them.

To Fargo all four looked a lot like Satan, black as could be, with long, slender necks and cropped combs and wattles.

Valle went to one of them and untied the rope that bound the first rooster's leg to the stake. She picked him up and held him close. Fargo didn't take to cuddling chickens, but he guessed it was all right for Valle to do it. The rooster seemed to like it, and Fargo didn't blame him.

Valle took the cock over to the run and opened the gate from the big pen into it with her free hand. She went into the run with the rooster and put him down. He stood there looking around while Valle closed the gate.

When the gate was closed, Valle flapped her hands and made a clicking noise with her tongue. The rooster started to run, and Valle ran along behind him, encouraging him to run faster. They got to the other end of the run, turned around, and came back.

"I see why she calls it a 'run,'" Calder said.

Valle chased the cock up the run and back four times. Then she repeated the process with the other three cocks. When she was finished, Calder said, "I knew you was gonna use 'em in a fight, but I didn't know there was gonna be a race."

Valle laughed. "There's no race. We do that to strengthen their legs. The legs are the most important part of a fighting cock. Without strong legs, he doesn't stand a chance."

"Be good for me in a fight, too," Calder said. "Help me run away faster."

"You didn't run yesterday," Valle pointed out.

"Yeah," Calder admitted. "That was a big mistake. I've learned my lesson now."

"I don't think you have," Valle said.

"How come you don't get 'em to fightin'?" Calder wondered. "Looks to me like you'd want 'em to learn some of that."

"They don't need any training for that. It's natural to them. They don't mind people being around them or holding them, but they don't like each other. If they weren't staked out in the pen, there'd be a new fight breaking out every five minutes. It's just the way they are."

"Not so different from people, then, are they?" Calder said.

Valle gave him a rueful grin. "Maybe not. You want to help me feed and water them?"

"Sure. How about you, Fargo?"

The Trailsman allowed as how he'd be glad to help out, and before long the job was done. Then they went to where the hens were penned to do the same chore and gather the eggs.

"Ain't nothin' smells like a chicken yard," Calder said. "Be careful where you step, Fargo."

Fargo wasn't worried about getting chicken shit on his boots. He was worried about what he was going to do about the bank robbers.

The bank robbers knew what they were going to do about Skye Fargo, however.

They pounded full tilt into Roseburg in the middle of the morning, bold as the newly polished brass buttons on a soldier's uniform. Nothing distracted attention from them. In fact, it was as if they were trying to *draw* attention to themselves. They rode in shouting and whooping, waving their hats and firing their pistols into the air, scattering people in the street and chasing dogs under the boardwalk.

All the men in the gang had bandannas pulled up to conceal their faces, except one man who rode in the lead. He had a neatly trimmed beard and wore fringed buckskins. He shouted orders to the others, and they reined to a halt in front of the bank. The dust they'd raised settled over them as the men jumped down from their mounts.

They didn't have a chance to get much farther than that, however. Men with pistols began firing on them. Shopkeepers armed themselves and fired as well. Bullets chipped off bits of wall and plowed up dirt, but no one was hit.

The robbers mounted up even faster than they'd

gotten out of the saddle, and at a word from their leader they spurred away, returning fire but not to much effect other than causing the men behind them to duck for cover.

As soon as the outlaws were out of range, the men moved back into the street.

"Damn," said one man as he watched the receding backs of the riders. "Look at the sons of bitches run!"

"That bunch is gettin' downright audacious," someone else said. "Comin' in here like that when ever'-body's in town and ready to fight back. I guess we showed 'em they can't rob a bank in Roseburg like they can somewheres else."

"Damn right! We scattered 'em. They'll think twice before they mess with us again."

"Did you see that'un in the lead? Didn't even bother to cover his face. Like he thought nobody'd ever see him again. He'll sure be easy to spot in that getup he had on. He better never show his face around this town no more."

"Nor anywhere else. Now that we got a good look at him, he's bound to wind up in jail pretty quick."

"Too bad for him he got so careless."

"Damn right. He's gonna regret that for a long time to come."

After a while, the men drifted back to their usual pursuits. They didn't consider going after the gang. They couldn't have caught them, and they were satisfied having driven them away and having taught them that no bank robbers better mess with Roseburg.

That afternoon Fargo asked Valle to ride into Roseburg and find out what the news was about the robbery in Ashland. Mainly he wanted to know if there was any news about somebody fitting his description being involved.

"You wouldn't have to ride the mule," he said. "You could take Tom's horse."

Valle agreed, though she was reluctant to leave. Maybe she didn't think anyone would be there when she got back.

After she'd gone, Fargo and Calder sat on the porch on a couple of upended nail kegs and smoked while they talked things over.

"The way I see it," Calder said, blowing a smoke ring that wavered and floated away, "you're about to get the two of us in big trouble. If we let Wolf and his boys get away with another robbery that we know about in advance, we're just about as guilty as he is."

"Who's going to tell we knew?" Fargo said.

"You got a point there," Calder said with a nod. "Sure won't be me."

"We can track them after they leave town," Fargo said. "Find out where they're hiding and let the marshal do the rest of the job."

"Maybe you can track 'em. I don't doubt it. So why not just lead the posse?"

"I might. It depends on what Valle finds out."

"Make it a lot easier if we did it that way."

Fargo knew Calder was right, but if the word had been spread that the Trailsman was the leader of the gang, it would be impossible to go to the law.

And it turned out that the word had spread, all right. When Valle returned and told them what she'd learned in Roseburg, the news was worse than Fargo had imagined it might be.

Valle told them how Fargo had led the gang into town and tried to rob the bank there only that morning.

"Damn," Calder said. "You really do get around, don't you, Fargo? Here I thought you were with me all the time, and you're out robbin' banks on the sly."

Fargo didn't think it was quite as funny as Calder seemed to find it.

"They didn't get anything, though," Valle said. "They

56

got chased off before they could even get inside the bank. And it couldn't have been you, could it?"

No, it couldn't have been Fargo, who decided that Wolf was smarter than the Trailsman had given him credit for being. He'd had one of his men dress like Fargo and then pulled off a feint at the bank to let half the town have a look at him. Maybe Wolf had been the one. If he'd trimmed his beard and worn buckskins, it would have been easy enough.

Whatever he'd done, Wolf had made sure that Fargo wouldn't be getting any help from the law, and he'd also found himself a handy scapegoat for all the robberies. Nobody would be looking for Wolf. They'd all be hunting for someone who looked and dressed like Skye Fargo.

"I guess this means we'll have to catch that Wolf fella all by our lonesomes," Calder said.

Fargo nodded. "I guess it does."

"I sure hope you can come up with a good idea."

"I have until Saturday," Fargo said. "Plenty of time."

"It better be," Calder said.

The next day Fargo was up early again. Nobody would ever sleep late with all those roosters bragging about helping the sun come up. After breakfast Valle ran the four cocks, and Fargo and Calder helped with the feeding.

"Who's gonna take care of doin' this while we're gone?" Calder asked.

He tossed out a handful of corn that the clucking chickens clustered around him pecked at eagerly.

"You gotten fond of being a chicken rancher?" Fargo asked. "Maybe you'd like to stick around."

"I ain't tryin' to get out of goin' with you. I just didn't want 'em to starve to death."

"I talked to Pete Folsom who lives on the way to town," Valle said. "He'll come by and do the feeding and egg gathering. He's going to let me borrow his wagon, too. He'll bring it in the morning."

"What if he's heard about the robbery?" Fargo said. "That might be a little chancy."

"He won't have heard. He hasn't been to town."

"We can't be usin' a wagon, anyway," Calder objected. "We'd have to use the main trail."

"We can't go without the cocks," Valle said. "And we can't take them unless we have a wagon."

"Just can't do it," Calder said. "Not with people on the lookout for Fargo the way they are." He turned to look at the Trailsman. "Not too many folks around look like him."

"That's the truth," Valle said.

Her admiring tone must have irked Calder. "That ain't the way I meant it. I mean he don't dress like normal folks."

"He could do something about that."

"What could I do?" Fargo said, though he was afraid he already knew what she was going to tell them.

"Wear some different clothes. Shave your beard."

Exactly what Fargo had expected. He shook his head and said, "I'll have to think about that."

"Think hard," Calder said. "And be thinkin' about that plan of yours, too."

"What plan?" Valle said.

"That's the trouble," Calder said. "There ain't one."

That night Valle was more avid than before in her lovemaking, not that she'd been shy up until then. As soon as Calder's snores began to rise in volume, she climbed into the bed with Fargo and grasped his already erect member.

"You're not the kind to ever settle down in one place, are you, Skye?" she asked.

Fargo didn't feel much like answering the question, considering the grip she had on him. He felt even less like answering when she lowered her head and kissed the tip.

He hoped she'd forgotten having asked, but she raised up and said, "Well?"

"I'm not that kind," Fargo said.

"I never thought you were." Valle's clever fingers worked up and down his shaft as softly as butterfly feet. "I know you'll be moving along as soon as you help me get Pa back. You are going to help me, aren't you, Skye?"

Fargo was breathing a little harder than normal because Valle's fingers had now encircled his shaft and begun moving rapidly up and down.

"I'm going to help you," he said.

He wanted to add that he'd most likely have helped her even if she hadn't gotten in bed with him, but he was beyond doing much talking.

"I was scared," she said. "And afraid. You made me feel better about everything. I'll always remember that, even if you leave."

"Uh," Fargo said.

"You like that?"

"Uh."

Valle released him, then straddled him. She lowered herself toward his stiff manhood, grasped it again, and rubbed it on her swollen nether lips. She sighed and inserted the tip of the hardness into her wet opening, still teasing Fargo, whose breath came faster than ever.

With a quick twist of her hips, Valle took him all the way inside her, surrounding him with the hot dampness. She pressed down hard against him, pinning him to the bed while she squirmed above him.

Fargo let that go on for a while, allowing himself to enjoy the sensation to its fullest. He felt his engorged organ swell even more, grow even harder, and at that point he put his hands on her waist and turned her over, with the result that he was now on top.

"Yes," she said. "Give it to me, Skye. Give me all you have."

Fargo gave it to her, slowly at first and then faster. She matched his strokes with the movement of her own hips, and soon they were writhing together in a synchronized dance that could have only one ending.

Valle's head was back, her mouth open, and she crammed a fist into it to stop what was about to become a scream of ecstasy.

Fargo took it as a signal and let himself go, pumping one steaming shot after another into her as her own orgasm wracked her entire body.

When it was over, they lay side by side in the narrow bed that could hardly hold the two of them. After a quiet moment or two, Valle said, "I know you're not helping me because of that. You're not that kind of man."

Fargo was glad she'd come to that realization, if she really had. He wasn't entirely sure he believed it. She'd manipulated him and Calder back in Ashland, getting them to the house while appearing reluctant for them to come. He wondered if he could really trust her.

At the moment, he didn't care. He'd worry about that later, if he had to. For now, he'd just enjoy her company and her favors.

He listened to Calder snoring in the other room for a minute or two, and then he fell asleep.

Pete Folsom turned out to be a young man not much older than Valle. He was brawny and awkward, with a sun-browned face and hands that had done a lot of work around a farm of some kind or other. And while Fargo had been wrong in thinking that Tom was sweet on Valle, there was no mistaking that Pete was. It was obvious in everything he did or said when he was around her.

"Better watch out," Calder said as he and Fargo sat

on the nail kegs and watched Valle showing Pete how to take care of the cocks. "That young fella's liable to beat your time."

"I think he already has," Fargo said.

Calder grinned evilly. "I wouldn't say that."

"What would you know about it?"

"I know what I know. I might snore like a locomotive engine, but I ain't dumb."

Fargo grinned, too. Calder's earlier jokes had made it clear that he knew what was going on.

"Speakin' of bein' dumb," Calder said, "you come up with that plan yet?"

"Not yet."

"Ain't even shaved off that beard, and we'll be leavin' pretty soon. What you gonna do about that?"

Fargo had considered shaving the beard, but he'd decided not to. Plenty of men had beards. He'd have to doff his buckskins, however. That was what most people would remember about the bank robber who was supposed to be him, so he was willing to go that far.

"Valle told me that her pa's clothes would fit me," he said. "I'm going to give them a try. I won't be shaving, though."

"Didn't think you would. If you're gonna try those clothes, you better get at it. We ain't gonna be here much longer."

Fargo stood up and went inside. There was a small trunk in the room where Calder had slept, and Fargo opened it up. Inside it were some well-worn wool shirts and a few pairs of equally worn denim pants. There was also an old Walker Colt, a bulky pistol that was hard to handle and didn't look as if it had been used much.

Fargo stripped off his own shirt and tried on one of Mr. Wilson's. It was a little tight through the chest, but it would do.

Unlike the shirt, the pants were a bit too big. They

were loose in the waist, but they'd also be all right if Fargo cinched up his belt. Fargo strapped his Arkansas toothpick to his leg, put on his gun belt, and stood still for a minute. He couldn't see himself, but he thought he looked different enough that nobody would think of him as the Trailsman.

He went back outside. Calder looked at him and said, "Who the hell are you, and what're you doin' here?"

"You do more hoorawin' than any man I ever met," Fargo said.

"Well, you do look different. Get you a hat on, and I think we might even be able to ride right into town without anybody botherin' us."

"We might, at that," Fargo said, but something about that fact bothered him. He couldn't figure out what it was, but Valle and Pete came to the porch before he could worry about it anymore.

"Pete knows what to do, and he has to be going home. We can load up the cocks and be on our way."

"You take care, Valle," Pete said.

He looked at Fargo when he spoke.

"I'll be fine," she said.

Fargo knew she hadn't told him the truth of the situation. He and Valle had talked it over and come up with a story. She'd told Pete that her father had gone ahead to Jacksonville and that she was joining him. Fargo and Calder were old friends of her father's who'd be traveling along with her.

How much of that Pete believed, Fargo didn't know. It didn't much matter. He was likely to go along with anything that Valle asked him to.

Pete went and unhitched the mule from his wagon. Unlike Valle, he didn't even bother with blankets. He was used to riding a mule bareback, Fargo supposed. He bid them good-bye and rode off, looking back a couple of times before he was out of sight.

"Fine young fella," Calder said. "You two make a nice pair."

"He thinks I'm going to marry him," Valle said.

"Are you?"

"It depends."

"Depends on what?" Fargo said.

"If we live through the next few days."

"I was telling Fargo that we could go to the law. He don't look like the gang leader now."

Valle appraised him. "He looks different, sure enough. The clothes don't fit as well as I thought, though. I underestimated him."

"Don't matter. We can still get to the law without anybody takin' a shot at us."

"You could try," Valle said. "But if you do, Wolf will kill my father."

"How's he gonna know?"

"He said he'd be leaving two men behind with Pa. If the gang didn't come back from the bank, those men were to kill Pa and leave him where he fell. I'll never see him again, not alive."

"Damn," Calder said. "I guess we should'a thought of that. How's that affect the plan, Fargo?"

"What plan?" Fargo said.

5

Wolf Jensen had a plan. That was one thing he prided himself on. He always had a plan.

Sometimes plans changed. That was all right, too, as long as the change was a good one, something that would work out in his favor.

That's the way it had happened in Ashland, thanks to the Brysons, who'd been taking care of things there for him.

Now the Brysons had joined the gang for the last big robbery, the bank in Jacksonville. Jensen thought he might need some extra men, and the Brysons would fit right in. They'd told their cousin, the marshal, that they wanted to keep on hunting for the gang so their disappearance from Ashland wouldn't look suspicious.

When the Brysons told him about the stranger who'd been at the cockfight and how they'd tried to throw the blame for the Ashland robbery on him, Wolf had immediately decided to make sure that the stranger— Fargo, his name was—got tied to another robbery attempt.

It was lucky that Jensen had a man named Joe Brody, who resembled Fargo slightly. The buckskin clothes were easy enough to come by, and Brody made sure everybody in Roseburg got a good look at him. They wouldn't remember much more than the beard and the buckskins, but that would be enough.

Brody would be riding as Fargo again, this time in the Jacksonville robbery later in the week. Not many would see him then, if Jensen's plans went right, but those who did see him would again remember the things Jensen wanted them to remember.

Fargo, whoever he was, would have a lot of sleepless nights worrying about the law after that, Jensen hoped. Besides those worries, Fargo would be spending some time in jail if he didn't disappear from this part of the country.

The idea of having someone else take the blame for his crimes pleased Jensen mightily, and he chuckled.

There was just one little problem. The Brysons had passed through Roseburg to see if Fargo had taken Valle Wilson back to her place. They'd spied on the house from a distance, and Valle was there, all right.

So was Fargo. But not Tom.

Jensen didn't worry much about what happened to his men. They could take care of themselves. They knew that was what they were supposed to do, but Tom had been left there to keep Valle in line, to make sure that she did her part in Jacksonville.

"It'll be all right," Patrick Wilson said. "Valle wouldn't be letting me down."

Valle's father was a big man, considerably bigger than his daughter, with the same fair hair, only his was beginning to turn gray. He sat beside Jensen at the entrance to the cave, smoking a battered pipe. Not far away, Big Boy, the Brysons, and the others were stirring a pot of rabbit stew over a fire. There wasn't much danger that anybody would see the smoke. Nobody ever came to that part of the country south of Jacksonville. As far as Wilson knew, nobody else was even aware that the cave was there.

It was halfway up a mountain, and the entrance was half covered by a slab of stone that had slid down from the top. Brush grew around the opening, and the stone itself was mostly covered with dirt in which green grass grew. Jensen had stumbled across the cave a year or so earlier while on the run from a posse, and he'd decided then and there that it would make the perfect place to hide out after robberies in neighboring towns. So far, he'd been right.

"You have a lot of faith in your daughter," Jensen said.

Wilson knocked the contents of his pipe out against a rock and stuck the pipe in his pocket.

"She wouldn't be wanting her old pa to die, now would she?" he said.

Wolf Jensen chuckled again. "I guess she wouldn't. You got the wool pulled right down over her eyes."

"It's nothing I want to be bragging about," Wilson said.

"You could just have told her the truth."

Wilson stared off over the countryside below. "Valle's too good to go along with your crooked schemes, knowing the truth of them. She takes after her mother, may God rest her soul."

Jensen and Wilson had met years before, when Wilson was working as a cardsharp in California during the gold rush. Wilson had been crooked but clumsy and was forced to seek better living conditions far away, and Oregon had seemed like a fine place. He'd saved enough money to spend his time raising cocks, and he'd made a bit more money with them, but not enough.

When Jensen had turned up one night in a saloon, they'd talked over old times, and Jensen had mentioned that he had a plan to make money, a lot of money, and that he might be able to use a little help. Wilson had listened and fallen in with the plan, though he'd known Valle would take some persuading. Wilson was the one who'd come up with the idea of pretending to be kidnapped.

Jensen patted his old pal on the shoulder. "As long as she does what she's supposed to do in Jacksonville on Saturday, I don't care why she's doing it. I just care that the job gets done."

"She'll get it done," Wilson said, sounding a bit sad about it. "You can believe that, for sure and for certain."

Jensen wasn't worried much about Valle. He was more worried about the stranger, Fargo. The way he'd jumped into the fight at the barn in Ashland said something about the man.

And there was Tom, a little hotheaded, but damned fast with a gun. If Fargo had taken Tom out of the picture, then Fargo might be a concern.

Valle wouldn't let him interfere with the robbery, though. Not as long as she thought her father's life was in danger. Hell, if they were lucky, Fargo would get picked up by the law and be taken out of the picture.

"I believe Valle will do just fine," Jensen said, standing up. "That rabbit stew smells good."

"Sure and it does," Wilson said. "Why don't we be having us a little of it now?"

The two men started toward the fire to join the others, Jensen with a smile on his face. Wilson walked a little behind him, not smiling, as if lost in thought.

Fargo, Valle, and Calder traveled the road to Jacksonville without encountering any trouble. The truth was that they saw so few people that they likely could have gone that way even if Fargo had been wearing his buckskins.

"I still think you oughta shave that beard," Calder said as they got nearer the town. "You'd be a whole sight less likely to draw attention."

"Lots of men have beards," Fargo said. "Anyway, nobody will even look at me. They'll all be looking at Valle."

They had decided that Valle wouldn't try to hide her identity this time, figuring that it would be less likely for anyone to associate her with the events in Ashland if she were to appear in Jacksonville as herself. There was no doubt that people in Jacksonville had heard about the bank robbery, but just how much they'd heard about Fargo, Valle, and Calder was an open question. Some people in Jacksonville knew Valle and her father, so the disguise might not work if she tried it.

"Couldn't blame folks for looking at Valle," Calder said. "We still gonna separate?"

"Might be a good idea. Even less of a chance of anybody connecting us to Ashland."

Besides, Fargo wanted a chance to prowl around the town with the possibility of finding out who Wolf's spies there were, assuming that the spies existed. Valle had mentioned them, but Fargo wasn't sure they would really be there.

Calder rode up beside the wagon that rolled along slowly behind the mule, its wheels making little ruts in the dust, its joints creaking as the dry wood rubbed together.

"What do you think of us separatin' before we get to town, Valle?" he said.

Valle glanced over at Fargo, who grinned at her.

"I suppose we have to," she said. "It's safer for all of us that way, and I can take care of the cocks without any help."

"Where you gonna keep 'em?"

"There's a man here who keeps gamecocks. Fred Torbett. He has a good pen, and he might let me keep the cocks with his if there's room. I'll ride out to his place and ask."

"Won't they try to kill each other?"

"No more than with any other cocks. If they're kept staked and separated, they'll be all right."

"Where will you stay?"

"With Fred and his wife. They're good friends of my father."

Fargo was curious about that. "Won't they wonder where he is?"

"I'll tell them that he's back at home and that he sent me here to get a little experience on my own. They'll believe that."

"How about exercisin' the birds?" Calder said.

"Fred has a good run. He'll be glad to let me use it, I'm sure. He'll probably even help me organize the cockfight. He knows everybody who'd be interested."

"You won't be fightin' his birds?"

Valle leaned forward, resting her forearms on her knees as she stared out beyond the upright ears of the mule.

"No. He and Pa are friends, and they might try their own birds out against each other for sport, but never in a real match. We'll need somebody who can bet good money to get people in town out to see it."

"You gonna put down any bets yourself?"

Fargo remembered that Valle had told him she'd made bets in Ashland, but that was before she'd confessed the real purpose of the cockfight. He didn't know if she'd been telling the truth.

But it appeared that she had. She said, "Yes. I have to make it look as if I really care about the outcome of the fight."

"You mean you don't?"

"No. I do care. A lot. I like to see our cocks win. But the people in town won't believe I care unless I bet. That way more of them will get interested and involved."

"You said you lost money in Ashland," Fargo said. "How much?"

"At least fifty dollars. I couldn't afford to lose that much. It was about all we had. I don't know what I'll do in Jacksonville. Maybe Fred will let me borrow some money."

"Hell," Calder said, "I'll do that. That is, I'll give it to you to bet for me. We can share the winnin's."

Calder reached over and patted one of the rooster cages on its top. The rooster didn't appear to be bothered.

"You sound mighty sure she'll win," Fargo said.

"If she's got another rooster like Satan, she will." Calder patted the cage again. This time the rooster fluttered its wings but nothing more. "How about it, Valle?"

"All right. It would be a help, and I can promise you'll get your money back, and more."

"Not if another fight breaks out," Fargo said. "What kind of extra distraction will you use this time?"

"I don't know. That fight wasn't my idea. That was the Brysons. I didn't know they'd be so upset by what Satan did. Things like that don't usually cause such a ruckus."

That made Fargo wonder about the Brysons. He should have thought about their part in the whole thing sooner. He wondered if the Brysons were somehow involved with the gang of bank robbers. Considering the ruckus they'd caused, it seemed possible.

They were coming into the outskirts of Jacksonville now, passing an occasional frame house sitting on a small patch of land among the big trees.

"We better hang back a little," Calder said, slowing his horse. "Let Valle go on through town without us. We can stop at a saloon and wet our whistles."

That sounded good to Fargo. He said his good-byes to Valle and dropped back beside Calder. As they watched the wagon move ahead, Calder said, "What about her, Fargo? You think she's on the up-and-up?"

"I'm not sure," Fargo said, surprised that Calder had asked.

"I don't like this whole thing about us not goin' to the law. I don't want to spend any time in jail."

"You were willing to bet money with her, so I figured you trusted her."

"I trust her to win. The rest of it worries me."

"Me, too," Fargo said.

The gold rush days were behind Jacksonville, and it had settled back into being just another small town. A small town, that is, with some very wealthy residents, because they'd made plenty from the gold strike. In fact, money was still coming in from some of those claims.

The Grizzly Bear Saloon looked like the best of the two in town. It wasn't crowded, and Fargo learned nothing there, other than the fact that nobody seemed interested in either him or Calder except for the fact that they were strangers in town.

To anybody who asked, Calder explained that they were partners who were hoping to strike a little color. While nobody outright laughed at him, Fargo saw a hidden smile or two, and one man nudged a friend and grinned. Fargo was glad to see the reaction because it meant that he and Calder were being taken for nothing more than another pair of crazy fools who believed there was still gold to be found and a fortune to be made.

They left the saloon after having a couple of drinks and rode out of town to make camp. Fargo didn't want to stay in a hotel.

That evening they sat at a little fire that crackled and popped in the sticks, sending pine-scented smoke twisting into the air.

"You got a plan yet?" Calder asked, leaning back against the bole of a tree. "Seems to me it's about time for one."

Fargo took a sip of coffee that tasted just a little too bitter. He wasn't sure if the coffee was the problem or if the situation added the bitterness to the brew.

"Seems to me it's been about time for one for a

couple of days now," Calder continued. "Believe you said you had that long to come up with one. Or maybe I'm wrong."

Fargo set his cup down on the ground and reached for his makin's. When he'd rolled a smoke and taken a puff, he said, "I have a plan."

Calder stretched up and down, scratching his back on the tree trunk.

"I'm mighty glad to hear it. You gonna tell me what it is?"

"Later," Fargo said.

"Damn it to hell, Fargo. You don't have any plan a'tall, do you?"

Fargo didn't answer. He had a plan, but it wasn't a very good one, and he didn't like anything about it. Half of it was something they'd already discussed, and he hadn't liked it the first time, either.

"I'm going to let the robbery go on as planned," he said. "Then I'm going to track the gang."

"And then whip their asses and take the money away from them, I guess," Calder said.

"Nope. After the robbery, we're going to ride with the posse. They might not be able to find Wolf and his men on their own, but maybe I can do the job for them. So I'll have help whipping their asses."

"That's the best you can do?"

"It's the best I can do. I don't want to get Valle's pa killed. Do you?"

"I sure don't." Calder tipped his hat down over his eyes. "I think I'll go to sleep now."

Fargo knew Calder couldn't sleep where he was, or not very well. But he didn't say anything. He finished his smoke and got his bedroll. He was going to sleep in comfort. Or as much comfort as his worries would allow him.

The next couple of days passed quickly. People in Jacksonville were talking about the cockfight. Fargo and Calder spent some time in the Grizzly Bear Saloon, listening to what they had to say, and that's when the trouble started.

"It ain't right for a woman to be doin' any cockfightin'," one lanky man said, leaning back against the bar with his elbows braced on it.

His comment got several nods and grunts of agreement.

"Women oughtn't even be allowed to watch," the lanky man went on. "Cockfightin' is a man's sport; always has been. We've had presidents who had gamecocks, and you can bet their wives didn't have a thing to do with any of it."

More agreement, louder this time. Fargo couldn't figure what the man's purpose was in getting people stirred up.

Then it occurred to him that maybe the man was the watcher that Wolf had left in town and that he was working on the crowd to get them more interested in the cockfight.

"Look out there," the man said, pushing himself away from the bar and pointing past the batwing doors at the front of the saloon.

Fargo looked and saw Valle standing on the boardwalk, talking to a bulky man wearing a frock coat, high-waisted pants, and a black cravat. Banker, Fargo thought, or maybe a lawyer.

"See how she's pushing herself on him?" the lanky man said. "Oughta be ashamed. Trying to set up some kind of a bet, you can count on it. Just not the kind of thing for a woman to be doing, the way I see it."

"What you gonna do about it, Earl?" someone said.

"By God, I'll do something. Don't you think I won't."

"Let's see you do it, then," came a voice from a table nearby.

A couple of men pounded their glasses on the table to show their agreement, and Earl started for the door. Chairs scraped the floor as men pushed away from the tables and stood up, waiting to see what Earl had in mind.

Calder looked at Fargo, who shook his head. He didn't want to get involved unless he had to. He didn't want to call any undue attention to himself.

Earl's boot heels clomped on the floor as the lanky man crossed to the batwings and pushed through them. A man standing near the doors grabbed one on the backswing and held it open so everyone inside could enjoy the action that they expected was about to begin.

Earl shoved himself between Valle and the man she was talking to. He stuck his finger under the man's nose.

"You look here, Kinkade, you oughta know better than to be talkin' to this woman. She's got no business gettin' up a cockfight in this town."

Kinkade pushed Earl's hand out of the way. "Step aside, Earl. You've had too much to drink."

Earl gave him a shocked look.

"Too much to drink? The hell you say. You can't tell me how much I oughta drink."

Earl hadn't seemed drunk at all to Fargo, who wondered if he was watching a little play being acted out.

If it was a play, Earl was taking it seriously. He backed up against Valle, shoving her out of the way as he wound up to hit Kinkade.

Winding up was a mistake. Kinkade simply reached out, took hold of Earl's arm, twisted it up behind Earl's back, and turned him around. Then he shoved Earl past the open door and back into the saloon.

Earl's arms windmilled as he stumbled forward and tried to keep his balance. He wasn't entirely successful, though he managed to dodge two tables before crashing into a third one, sending drinks flying and chairs skidding. He lay across the table, looking dazed.

Fargo looked outside and saw Valle give Kinkade

an admiring look. Kinkade was pleased as could be with that look. His chest puffed out, and he came into the saloon after Earl.

Earl got off the table and stared around wide-eyed, as if wondering what had happened to him. Kinkade came up behind him and plunked a heavy hand down on Earl's shoulder.

Earl turned, and Kinkade hit him with a short jab, sending Earl into the arms of a couple of men standing behind him. The men looked at each other, shrugged, and pushed Earl right back at Kinkade, who hit him again. Fargo heard something break, probably Earl's prominent nose.

This time the two men didn't bother to catch Earl. They moved aside and let him fly right past them. Another man moved a table out of the way, and Earl hit the side wall of the saloon. The little air he had left in him whoofed out, and Earl's eyes rolled up in his head. He slid down the wall and assumed a seat on the floor. His head lolled to one side, and a ropey string of spit and blood hung out of the corner of his mouth.

Well, if that was an act, Fargo thought, looking at Earl's battered face, it was a pretty convincing one.

Kinkade dusted his hands ostentatiously. Fargo thought for a second of the way the rooster Satan had hopped up on the body of General Washington, stuck out his chest, and crowed. Kinkade's chest swelled, and he looked as if he'd like to do the same thing with Earl.

Before he could, Valle came into the saloon and thanked him for defending her. Her eyes shone, and Fargo could tell that Kinkade was powerfully affected. He might have liked to hang around and get some compliments from the men on his fighting skills, but Valle had more allure, and he followed her out of the saloon and down the boardwalk.

"Who was that fella?" Fargo said to a man at the bar. "He's quite a fighter."

"Hell," the man said. He spit on the floor and rubbed it in with the toe of his boot. "That's Ben Kinkade. Owns the bank here in town. Thinks he's the bull moose if you ask me. Likes it when he can whip up on a fella."

Kinkade would have plenty of money to bet on the match, Fargo thought, and others would follow him. Valle was on the way to having everybody in town there at the cockfight, and she had the banker helping her. Fargo smiled.

"What's so funny?" Calder asked.

"Nothing," Fargo said, looking over at Earl, who was being helped to his feet by the two men who hadn't caught him the second time. "I was just wondering about what we saw there."

"Saw a man get his ass kicked," Calder said. "That's what we saw."

"Maybe," Fargo said, still wondering if there wasn't more to it than that.

Earl's friends helped him out of the saloon, and Fargo forgot about him for the moment while he listened to more talk about the cockfight. Quite a bit of interest had been aroused by the fisticuffs, and Fargo thought there'd be a good crowd. Just what the bank robbers wanted.

Just what Fargo wanted, too. He was already revising his plan.

Fargo thought it over, finished his drink, and told Calder it was time to go.

"Where to?" Calder asked.

"The bank," Fargo told him.

The Jacksonville bank didn't look much different from any other building in town. It was located between a barbershop and dry-goods store. The local marshal's office was at the other end of the settlement, which would be convenient for the bank robbers.

"What do you think?" Calder said.

Fargo and Calder leaned against the wall of a big

livery barn across the street from the bank. The sun shone on the wall, and Fargo could feel the warm wood through his slightly too-tight shirt. A couple of men walked past the front of the bank, but other than that the street was quiet.

"I think hardly anybody will be around here tomorrow," Fargo said. "They'll all be at the cockfight, and the robbers will have an easy job of it."

Calder rubbed his back against the wall as if scratching it.

"Something might go wrong," he said.

"Things have a way of doing that, time to time."

"Might mess up your plan."

"About that plan," Fargo said. "I've changed my mind about it."

"Don't you think it's a little too late for that?"

"No. I might even change it again."

"You gonna tell me about it?"

"Might as well," Fargo said, and he did.

6

Fred Torbett had a cockpit in a big old barn near his house, and that was where the fight was to be held. Fargo and Calder were there and ready for the grisly festivities to begin.

The bird Valle had chosen to enter was named Nero. He strutted around enough to convince Fargo that his name was well chosen, though his likeness to an emperor ended with that one characteristic.

His opponent was a big white cock called George, which Calder said wasn't much of a name for a fighter.

"Maybe he's named for General Washington," Fargo said. "The real one, not the gamecock."

"Oughta call him the general, then," Calder said. "Make more sense if they did. Be a bad omen, though, him havin' the same name as that cock Satan whipped in Ashland. Could call him President, I guess."

Fargo didn't think names made much difference. Both birds had broad breasts and seemed spirited enough. It wasn't the bird's name that would win the fight.

George's handler was a man named Calhoun. He had eyes that were too close together and a thin, blond mustache. His long, bony fingers roved over his bird with nervous, jerky motions as he readied him for the fight.

Valle was calm and, just as she had in Ashland,

leaned over her bird as if she were whispering in its ear. Fargo wondered what she might be telling it. Strategy for the fight? He should have asked her about that. After all, it didn't seem likely that a rooster would understand a single word. Maybe, though, it was the tone that mattered.

Fargo didn't have much interest in the preliminaries to the fight and paid them little attention. He was more concerned about who was there to see the two birds tangle.

Ben Kinkade walked around the barn talking to everyone and slapping backs, his chest puffed out the way it had been after his fight with Earl. Fargo decided that Kinkade was like that all the time, proud of himself and his position in life, as if he were the most important man in town. Most likely he was, owning the bank and all.

Earl was there, too, but he stood well off to one side of the crowd, seemingly not interested in the betting or in getting a seat in the grandstand. Fargo didn't blame him. This grandstand didn't look as substantial as the one in Ashland, and that one had collapsed all too easily.

Earl had a black eye, and his mouth was puffed and purple where Kinkade had smashed his lip. His nose was twisted slightly to one side, and Fargo knew it would sit a little off center from then on.

Fargo recognized a few other people he'd seen around the settlement or in the saloon, but he didn't know their names. He'd kept pretty much to himself and hadn't gotten to know any of the townspeople because he didn't want anyone connecting him with the robberies.

Early that morning, just after dawn, Fargo and Calder had ridden out to Torbett's place to talk to Valle about the fight. Fargo wanted to know what kind of distraction Valle was planning this time so he'd know what to watch for.

"I'm not planning anything," she said. Her golden hair glinted in the rays of the rising sun, and Fargo wished he'd been able to visit her in the night. "I think that something will happen, the same way it did in Ashland. I'll have to wait and see. I just hope nobody kills my birds this time."

"Fargo's got him a new plan," Calder said.

"A new plan?"

"Same as the old plan," Calder said.

Fargo grinned and shook his head. "Not quite, but close. We're not going to wait to track Wolf's bunch. We're going into town and follow him."

A look of panic crossed Valle's face. "He'll see you. He'll kill my father."

"You don't know Fargo," Calder said. "A ghost is noisy and easy to spot compared to him. Wolf won't know anybody's behind him."

"Are you sure it's safe?"

"He's not in the habit of killin' anybody in the towns he robs," Calder said. "He'll slip in and out quiet as he can. And we'll be right behind him. Safe as anything."

Valle didn't look convinced, but she nodded. "All right. I hope it works."

"It better," Calder said.

Fargo and Calder had left Torbett's place a little while after that, not sticking around to meet the owner. They rode a short distance away and waited among the trees until the crowd from Jacksonville started to arrive. Then they rode back to the barn where Fargo had taken up his position near the door, which was left open this time to accommodate any latecomers.

Lots of money was changing hands, and Kinkade left off his backslapping to do some heavy betting. Fargo assumed the banker's money was all going down on Nero, though he couldn't be sure.

This fight was to be conducted under somewhat different rules from the one in Ashland. Calhoun wanted three rounds of ten minutes, maybe because he didn't think his bird had the stamina for one long round. Valle agreed easily, and Fargo knew it was because she didn't care about the rules. She just wanted the fight to go on so the robbers could do their job and give her back her father.

That was assuming they'd actually make good on their promise. Fargo wasn't so sure they would. He had a feeling that men who robbed banks most likely couldn't be trusted to keep their word on other matters.

Fargo's thoughts were interrupted by the referee's cry of, "Pit your birds!"

Fargo didn't know who the referee was. He thought it might be Torbett, but he supposed it didn't matter. The cocks ran at each other, and Nero soared into the air a split second before George. All that running that Valle did with the birds seemed to have strengthened their legs and given them a slight advantage over their opponents, but George wasn't easy to get the best of. He somehow got his claws into Nero's lower feathers, and the two of them went down in a flurry of flapping and kicking that stirred up a storm of dust and dirt from the floor of the barn and brought forth cheers from the crowd.

The fighting went on for what seemed like quite a while to Fargo. There was a great loss of blood and feathers on each side, always greeted by shouts of encouragement or dismay from the spectators, depending on which way they had wagered, but neither of the cocks seemed able to get the advantage on the other for more than a moment.

The referee looked at a big railroad watch he held in his right hand, then stepped in and stopped the fight, declaring that the first round was over.

Valle and Calhoun gathered their birds and took them to opposite sides of the pit. Valle spoke into

Nero's ear, or at least into the area of where an ear would be if he had one. Fargo wasn't sure he'd ever seen a chicken's ear, not that he cared to.

"How you reckon it's goin'?" Calder said.

Fargo said he couldn't tell. "Are you worried about your money?"

"I'm always worried about my money," Calder said. " 'Course, I just wanted to help Valle out—that's all."

"Right," Fargo said.

The referee ordered the handlers to pit their birds, and Calhoun and Valle returned to the center of the pit. This time Nero got a better jump, got above George, and drove a spur into the side of the other bird's neck.

A cheer went up from more than half the crowd, the ones who'd bet on Nero, Fargo figured.

The wound to George wasn't mortal. It was hardly even a deep one, but there was a good show of blood when George jerked away and scuttled to the side of the ring. Nero went right after him and soared up a foot or so before landing on him and digging furiously with spurs that flashed in the dim barn light.

The cheering and yelling from the crowd got louder and louder with every blow Nero struck.

It didn't take long after that. Calhoun's bird was down for good. It flapped away a couple of feet, but it couldn't rise, and Nero moved in for the sure kill.

Calhoun didn't let it happen. He ran over and grabbed his bird, clutching it to his chest, and declared that he'd concede the fight.

That didn't make anybody happy. The yells turned nasty and hateful. The men who'd bet on George wanted to see it through, and the others wanted to see a decisive victory. They wanted blood on the dirt.

Valle started talking to the man who was holding her money, and Calder grinned. He started to walk toward her, but Fargo put a hand on his shoulder and stopped him.

Calder looked at the Trailsman, who shook his head. "Not yet."

"Why not?"

"We don't know her. Wouldn't do to go taking money from her right now."

"Oh, yeah. I forgot."

Kinkade had no such worries. He was going around taking money from several hands, grinning and glad-handing, and that was when Earl made his move. He'd been leaning against a wall at one side of the barn, and he pushed away, heading for Kinkade at a limping jog.

"You owe me some of that money, Kinkade," he said. "You can't beat me like your dog and not pay me something for the privilege."

Kinkade looked at Earl, shoved some money in his pockets, and laughed.

"You're crazy as a one-eyed mule, Earl Langley. You should keep your mouth shut, and then you wouldn't get in trouble."

"I'll show you who's crazy," Earl said, swinging a balled fist at Kinkade's head.

Kinkade ducked aside and kicked Earl in the knee. Earl went down with a cry of pain, but not before he grabbed hold of a man nearby, pulling him down as well.

Confusion about what was going on caused some milling around and yelling, and then someone else hit a man and made a grab for his winnings.

"Here we go again," Calder said.

"That's right," Fargo said. "Time for us to get out of here."

"I guess I can't get my money from Valle, then."

"You guess right," Fargo told the old-timer. "Come on."

They'd been standing near the door, and they slipped out without being seen. Everyone was concentrating on the fight that had erupted and would soon involve everyone in the barn.

Fargo and Calder wouldn't be there to pull Valle out from under this time, as they'd warned her earlier. They were going to the bank to follow the robbers.

If they weren't already gone.

Wolf Jensen's gang wasn't likely to be gone quite as quickly as Fargo thought they might, and not nearly as quickly as Jensen had planned. The bad thing about having a plan was that sometimes things went wrong.

Sometimes it was little things. Sometimes it wasn't. But it was never things you could do anything about. Not things you could even imagine would happen.

This time it was a town marshal who didn't like cockfighting. Jensen had never heard of one like that before. In his experience, town marshals liked to be in on the action, and if everybody else in the place was out at some barn watching a couple of roosters kill each other, that's where the marshal would be as well. He might be making a bet or two, or he might just be there to keep an eye on things to see that they didn't get out of hand, as they often did at a cockfight. Whatever the reason, he'd be there.

That's the way it had worked in the past, and Jensen was sure it would be the same in Jacksonville.

But it wasn't. The marshal had stayed in his office. That had been the first thing that went wrong, though Jensen didn't know it yet.

The second thing was the bank teller. Tellers were supposed to follow orders when they saw a gun. The money wasn't theirs, and in this case the owner of the bank wasn't there to order anybody to protect it. A sensible teller should just give up the money without putting up any kind of a fight. The other tellers had.

But the teller in Jacksonville wasn't sensible. He had to be brave.

"Mr. Kinkade's not here," the teller said. He had thin, brown hair combed down so tight and close to the white skull that Jensen could see where the sparse strands didn't cover it. "He's the only one who can open the vault."

Jensen sure hadn't expected that kind of spine in the teller. He'd have bet that Kinkade hadn't expected it, either.

"The damn vault is already open," Big Boy told him. His voice was muffled by the bandanna he'd pulled up over his face, but the .44 he thrust under the teller's nose made his threat clear enough. "And if it ain't open already, you can open it. You take us to it."

The teller drew himself up. Even at his full height, he was a head shorter than Big Boy.

"You can kiss my ass," the teller said.

"You little turd," Big Boy said, and shot him twice in the chest.

The teller looked mightily surprised as he dropped to the floor, though Jensen didn't think he'd had time to be surprised before he died.

"God save us," Patrick Wilson said.

"Shitfire," Hap Bryson said.

"Shut up," Big Boy said. He shoved the dead teller aside with one foot. The body left a bloody smear on the floor. "Anybody else want to get smart with me?"

The one customer shook his head, and the other teller said nothing. He just stood where he was, shivering like a scared dog. The front of his pants sported a dark stain because he'd pissed them, and his teeth chattered.

"I didn't think so," Big Boy said with the satisfaction of a man who'd proved his natural superiority. "Now let's get the money."

Jensen just shook his head. He was sorry he'd ever taken Big Boy into the gang. They could have gotten the money without shooting anyone, which was the way Jensen preferred it. No use getting people riled up over a killing if you didn't have to, but Big Boy had always had a bad temper, and he had a bad habit of talking too much. Now Wolf was afraid it was going to cause them trouble.

And sure enough it did. They'd gotten to the vault, which was open just as Jensen had thought it would be, and started cleaning it out, cramming gold and coins into leather saddlebags, when Joe Brody, who'd been left to guard the front door, stepped inside and announced that someone was coming down the street to the bank.

Brody wore his fringed buckskins and the shivering teller got a good look at him, which at least was according to the plan.

"Who is it?" Jensen asked Brody.

"Looks like it might be the marshal."

"Damn it," Jensen said. "You make sure."

Brody went out and took a look.

It was the marshal, all right, and he had a couple of men with him. He must have heard the gunshots, or someone else had and sent for him.

"Shitfire," Hap said again when Brody gave them the news. "What're we gonna do?"

"How far off is he?" Jensen asked Brody.

"Not far enough, about three streets away is all."

"Be sure he gets a good look at you," Jensen told Brody, even though the teller and the customer had taken a good look already. "We want him to remember you."

"I'm not so sure I do," Brody said.

"What about us?" Hap said.

"Get the rest of the money," Jensen told him. "And be damn quick about it."

Hap ran to join his brother, Willie, who was in the

vault along with Big Boy, Wilson, and three others. When they came out of the back room into the bank, they were weighted down with saddlebags thrown over their shoulders.

"Is that it?" Jensen said.

"Much as we can carry," Wilson said, "and have our gun hands free."

"Then let's get out of here," Jensen said.

They left by the bank's front door while the marshal was still a block away. It was too bad that they'd planned to ride out of town in that direction.

Too bad for the marshal and his companions, that is. Jensen had no intention of changing his plan again.

The robbers tossed the bulging saddlebags onto their horses behind the saddles and mounted up. The marshal started running toward them.

"Ride the son of a bitch down if he gets in the street," Jensen said. "If he doesn't, shoot him. Take the lead, Brody. Let's ride!"

Brody put his spurs to his horse's sides and took off. The marshal fired a shot and ducked into an alley. The two men with him did the same.

Brody fired back. His bullet struck the edge of the building where the marshal had taken cover, sending splinters flying. Then the whole gang began to shoot into the air and at the buildings. Glass shattered. Chunks of wood jumped off the walls.

The gang whooped and hollered as they passed the marshal, who got off only a couple of shots at them, hitting nobody. The men with him hadn't yet managed to draw their pistols.

Jensen figured he was out of trouble and on his way.

But something else went wrong with his plan.

Something went wrong with Fargo's plan, too.

"You hear that shootin'?" Calder said as they neared town. "Bound to be Wolf."

Fargo figured Calder was right.

"What're we gonna do about it?" Calder said.

Fargo wished he had a good answer. He hadn't planned to get into anything with the gang right here and now. He'd simply wanted to follow them out of town, find out where they were hiding, and figure out a way to get Valle's father back. If he got the money back, too, that would be fine, but if he didn't, Calder would be able to put a posse on the right track. But it didn't seem that was going to happen.

"Let's see what's going on," Fargo said, and they urged their mounts forward.

When they arrived at the edge of town, they saw the gang galloping straight toward them, guns blazing.

Because it wasn't easy to hit a target, even a sizeable target, from the hurricane deck of a fast-moving horse, especially with a pistol, Fargo thought he was pretty safe for the moment.

He reined the big Ovaro to a halt and palmed his Colt from its holster. Calder stopped beside him and drew his own pistol.

Fargo raised the revolver, steadied himself, and pulled the trigger. His first shot knocked a bearded, buckskin-wearing hombre out of the saddle, sending him crashing to the ground. His second winged a man Fargo recognized as Willie Bryson, confirming his guess that the Bryson brothers were part of the gang and probably had been all along. Willie jerked in the saddle as Fargo's lead found him, but he was able to stay in the saddle.

Meanwhile Calder managed to shoot off Big Boy's hat.

Then the riders were on them, tearing past in a thunder of dust and horseflesh, bumping Fargo and Calder, but holding their fire now for fear of hitting one of their own.

As soon as they were past, they turned to sling lead again, but Calder and Fargo had ridden off the road. No bullets even came close to them, though with a carefully aimed shot Fargo managed to bring down one more of the gang members, whose foot caught in the stirrup as he fell from his horse. He bounced along beside the big animal for twenty or thirty yards, each bump raising a little dust cloud, before his foot came loose and he lay twitching in the middle of the road.

"We goin' after 'em?" Calder asked as the robbers dwindled in the distance.

"Not yet. Let's see if either of those men I shot can tell us anything."

"I think I got that second one," Calder said. "Hit him right betwixt the shoulder blades."

"Right," Fargo said, not seeing any use in argument. "Good shooting."

Calder nodded to acknowledge the compliment. "I wonder if there's a reward."

"Probably not," Fargo said.

He turned the Ovaro and rode to where the first man lay.

"Deader'n a hammer," Calder said as they looked down at him. There was a hole near the center of the man's chest with a dark bloodstain around it. "That's got to be the varmint they was passin' off as you. I don't think he looks much like you, though. Kind of a handsome feller, not that you ain't. You damn sure ruint his buckskins."

Fargo wasn't interested in the man if he was dead. He pulled on the Ovaro's reins and went to look at the other bank robber. He was dead, too, and considerably the worse the wear for having been dragged along the road.

"Looks a little like a wolf's been after his face," Calder said. "He ain't gonna tell you nothin'."

Fargo didn't reply.

The marshal came out of the alley where he'd taken cover and hurried toward Fargo and Calder. The other two men headed for the bank.

"We gonna go ahead and join up with the posse like we talked about?" Calder asked.

Fargo shook his head. "It'll take them too long to get organized. By the time they get the trouble at the cockfight sorted out, it'll be late afternoon. The posse might not even leave until the morning. We don't have that much time to waste. We'd better get started right now."

"I reckon we could catch up to 'em. Them horses looked loaded down to me."

The marshal arrived at that moment. He had a thin face, sunken cheeks, and big yellow teeth. He asked who Fargo and Calder were. Calder said he lived down in Ashland, and Fargo said he was visiting his friend. He didn't see any need to go into it further.

The marshal thanked them for what they'd done, and Fargo decided not to mention that they'd known about the robbery in advance. He didn't think the marshal would take that information too kindly.

"That's the same gang of owlhoots that's been robbing banks all around here," the star packer said. "Just a matter of time until they got to us, I reckon."

"Check the saddlebags on the horses the two we shot were riding," Fargo said. "Might be something in them that the bank's depositors will be glad to see."

"I'll do that. You two want to ride in a posse tomorrow?"

"We're going after them right now," Fargo said. "If you catch up with us, you can help us out."

He didn't think there was much chance of either thing happening.

"What're you planning to do if you catch up to those bastards?" the marshal asked.

"Don't ask him that," Calder said.

The marshal pushed back his hat and scratched his head.

"Why not?" he said.

" 'Cause he don't never have a plan. Ain't that right?"

"That's right," Fargo said.

"I wouldn't recommend that you go after that bunch on your own," the marshal said. "There's a lot of 'em, and they're mean as snakes."

"Less of 'em now than there was," Calder pointed out.

"Can't argue with that. I won't try to stand in your way if you want to make a chase. Just don't interfere with my posse if we come along after you."

"We won't do that," Fargo said.

"Good luck, then," the marshal said.

He turned around and went to see what had happened at the bank. Fargo and Calder rode off in the direction the bank robbers had taken.

The trail the gang left was an easy one to follow. The horses were carrying extra weight, and Jensen's men weren't making any effort to conceal their tracks. It bothered Fargo a little that they were so careless.

"Could be they ain't worried about a posse," Calder said as they rode through the thick trees. "Didn't anybody chase 'em after the Ashland robbery. Well, not for very long, anyway."

Fargo didn't respond.

"Or it could be that they have some kind of a plan," Calder continued. "Some folks do, you know."

Fargo said that he knew. He was bothered because he had a feeling that someone was following them. It was nothing he could explain, and he didn't see or hear anything when he stopped and looked over his shoulder down their back trail.

"You think the marshal's got a posse together already?" Calder asked after Fargo paused to look back for a second time.

"Not likely," Fargo said. "But there's somebody back there."

"I sure don't see 'em."

"Neither do I."

"Might make a man wonder if there was really anybody back there if it was anybody but you claimin' it."

"I could be wrong," Fargo said, although he didn't think he was. "Just don't let your guard down."

"No chance of that," Calder said.

7

Willie Bryson wasn't doing so well. He slumped to the side as he rode, and once he would have slipped off the saddle and fallen to the ground if Hap hadn't been right beside him to brace him up.

"Shitfire," Hap said. "Willie ain't gonna make it if we don't stop and see about that bullet that's in him."

"We're not stopping," Wolf said. "We're going to the cave. You can stop if you want to, but we're taking the saddlebags with us."

"You could at least give us our share," Hap said with a whine in his voice.

"We don't have time to divide it. I'll give you something from one bag. That's all. I'd do more, but we've already lost what Brody and Everts had."

Hap thought it over and said that would do. He got Willie's horse stopped and his own beside it.

"Take care of the split, Big Boy," Wolf said.

Hap drew his pistol. "Not that I don't trust you, Wolf, but if you mess around, I'll have to plug you."

Wolf grinned. His teeth hardly showed in the thicket of his beard.

"I'm sorry you don't trust me, Hap."

"No hard feelin's, I hope."

"Not a one. I can understand your thinking."

Big Boy pulled the saddlebags off both horses and took most of the money and gold, transferring what was in Hap's bags to the already loaded bags on the other horses. He took most of Willie's as well. It didn't take him long. He put Willie's and Hap's bags with what was left back on the horses.

"Be seeing you," Hap said, holstering the pistol.

"I doubt it," Jensen said as he rode away.

Hap didn't give a damn if he never saw Jensen again. He'd never liked the man, anyway. He and Willie could take care of themselves. That is, they could if Willie was all right, which seemed mighty doubtful.

Hap rode up the trail a ways, leading Willie's horse, until he saw a spot he liked behind some heavy brush. He angled his horse in that direction, and when he thought he was well concealed, he stopped to help Willie out of the saddle.

Willie didn't need any help. He slid right into Hap's arms. His shirt was wet and bloody.

"Shitfire," Hap said. "You ain't lookin' so good, Willie boy."

Willie had nothing to say to that. His eyes were closed, and his head lolled to one side.

"We should'a stuck to cockfights, Willie," Hap said with a catch in his voice, though he wasn't sure his brother could hear him anymore. "I'm sorry as hell we ever got talked into robbin' banks."

Hap overlooked the fact that nobody had talked them into anything. They'd practically begged to join the gang after Jensen had gotten in touch with them about the cockfight in Roseburg. They liked the idea of getting their hands on a lot of easy money.

Hap eased Willie to the ground and patted the saddlebag. At least they had some money to show for it. Not as much as they'd hoped, maybe, but more than they'd ever earned before. Plenty more than any cockfight had ever brought them.

And Willie *was* going to pull through. Hap was certain of it.

He was a lot less sure when he started to take Willie's shirt off. The bullet had gone into his chest, and now that Hap noticed it, Willie's breathing didn't sound so good. It was all ragged and whistling, which was odd because Willie hardly seemed to be breathing at all.

Hap saw the problem when he removed the shirt. Blood bubbled in the sparse hairs on Willie's chest, and that's where the whistling sound was coming from.

"Shitfire," Hap said. "A damn chest wound."

Willie didn't respond or even open his eyes. He wasn't going to pull through, after all. He wasn't going to last more than an hour, not without a doctor, and there wasn't any chance of finding one of those. Willie probably wouldn't make it even with a doctor's help.

Hap sighed. Those bastards had killed Willie. Who were they, anyway? They'd looked familiar.

Hap thought about the two men. He'd been concentrating on saving his ass instead of trying to get a good look at whoever was shooting at him, but now that he'd taken some time to reflect, he was sure that one of the bastards was Dodge Calder, that old man who lived close to Ashland. Hap didn't know the other one, but he'd looked a little like Joe Brody, which meant he might be the man who'd been with Calder at the fight in Ashland. What the hell was he doing in Jacksonville? Jensen had said he wouldn't dare show his face, what with folks thinking he was the leader of the bank-robbing gang.

The whistling sound came to an abrupt stop. Hap looked down at Willie. His head had turned to the side, and he was dead for sure now.

"Shitfire," Hap whispered.

He and Willie had been living together ever since they were kids and raising gamecocks for most of that time, eking out a living, such as it was, by gambling and selling some of their stock now and then. Now Willie was gone. Hap wondered what he was going to do.

Then he thought about the money in the saddlebags, money that he'd planned to split with Willie. Willie wasn't going to need his split, so Hap would have it all. He didn't know how much it was, but it would take him a long way from where he was, maybe down to California, where he could start over. Find a wife. He'd never had much chance of that with Willie always being around, but now he'd be quite a catch, what with his money and his natural good looks. Maybe he could find some nice-looking widow woman who could cook. Willie never could cook worth a damn.

Hap grinned. Maybe things weren't going to turn out so bad after all.

He figured he should bury Willie, but then he decided he didn't have time. He wanted to get started for California right away, and it wouldn't matter any to Willie whether he was lying on top of the ground or under it, not anymore.

"You see how it is, don't you, Willie?" Hap said. "You'd do the same if you was in my boots."

Willie didn't reply. His hat had come off and lay to one side. Hap picked it up and dropped it over his brother's face. He thought Willie looked more peaceful that way.

Hap would've said a few words from the Good Book if he'd known any. Since he didn't, he said nothing more. He took the reins of Willie's horse in one hand and put his foot into the stirrup of his saddle. He was halfway mounted when he remembered Calder and the man who was with him.

Hap stepped back down. What if those two were on his trail right now? It wouldn't do to let them catch up with him, not now that he was about to go to California and get hitched to a widow woman.

Hap looked around. He was pretty well hidden in the brush. He figured he could delay his start for California for a few hours under the circumstances. He'd just wait a while and then pick off whoever came riding along. Then the way would be clear. He couldn't bury Willie, though, even if he wasn't leaving yet. He had to keep a watch on the trail so nobody would get past him.

He tied the horses to a bush, found himself a good spot, pulled his pistol out, and settled down to wait.

"They stopped here for some reason," Fargo said, indicating the tracks on the ground.

"Hell, even I can see that," Calder said, "and I ain't no Trailsman. Not by a long shot. Looks like they went right on, though."

"A couple of them didn't," Fargo said. He pointed ahead to where Hap had ridden into the brush. "They might be waiting for us in there."

"Might be a good idea if we didn't ride into an ambush," Calder said. "I'd just as soon get back home with my skin all in one piece if it's just the same to you. What you think we oughta do?"

"Go back a little way and wait a while," Fargo said. "I hear somebody coming."

"I sure as hell don't. But I believe you."

"Come with me, then."

Fargo turned back down the trail they'd been following, and Calder, after a brief hesitation, started after him.

Fargo didn't go more than ten yards before turning aside into the trees, and by that time even Calder could hear the rider who was pursuing them.

"Kinda pushing it hard, ain't he?" Calder said. "You want me to shoot him?"

Fargo didn't make any comments on Calder's marksmanship. He said, "Might be better to see who it is, first."

"Oh," Calder said, as if that hadn't occurred to him. "Yeah. Might be better, at that. It's prob'ly Earl Langley, though, comin' for his part of the take." They had talked it over on the ride out here and were convinced that Earl was part of the gang. He had started that brawl at Torbett's barn on Wolf's orders.

Fargo nodded, but he was far from sure the rider following them was Earl. He could think of another possibility.

They didn't have long to wait to find out. Valle's mule came pounding along the trail, moving at a good clip, faster than a lot of horses would have been able to travel over that ground.

"I'll be damned," Calder said. "Never expected to see her out here. Better stop her before she rides into that ambush that's waitin' up there."

Fargo didn't think yelling would do any good, so he slid out his Colt and fired a shot into the air. The noise caused Valle to pull back hard on the reins.

The mule stood straight up, kicked its front legs in the air and dropped Valle out of the saddle. Which was a good thing, as the bullet that came out of the trees just then might well have hit her if she'd stayed on her course.

The mule ran off along the trail and disappeared around a bend. Valle rolled over a couple of times and wound up behind a tree trunk. As Fargo watched, she drew a huge Walker Colt from somewhere. Holding it with both hands, she aimed it and pulled the trigger. The pistol's impressive recoil forced her hands up and almost flipped her onto her side.

Fargo couldn't see where the shot went, and he didn't hear any result. He watched as Valle got herself into position again, but this time she didn't shoot. She remained still, watching the brush from which the shot at her had come.

"You just gonna sit there?" Calder said.

Fargo looked at him. "I believe that's what you said to me at that cockfight in Ashland, the one that got us into this mess in the first place."

"That ain't what I said."

"Close enough."

"And I didn't get us into any mess. You had as much to do with it as I did."

"Right," Fargo said.

"Don't matter who did what, anyway," Calder said. "You can't just let Valle get picked off."

Fargo supposed Calder had a point. "You stay here. I'll see if I can slip around in back of whoever's doing the shooting."

"You better let Valle know we're here 'fore you go slippin' anywhere. You don't want to get shot with that cannon of hers. Bullet from that thing goes in your belly, your backbone'd end up back in town." Calder paused. "Wonder where she got a gun like that."

"Out of a trunk," Fargo said. He was a little peeved because he hadn't seen Valle sneak it into the wagon when they'd left. "Belongs to her pa, I guess. You let her know I'm around."

Calder might have discussed the pistol some more, but Fargo was already gone, sliding off the big Ovaro and into the trees so quietly that Calder didn't even realize it had happened.

Calder dismounted and walked to a tall pine with a trunk big enough to conceal most of his body. He stuck his head around the trunk and hissed at Valle a couple of times until she looked around, pointing the Colt in his direction.

"It's just me," he said. "Dodge Calder. Fargo's here, too. Don't go shootin' at us."

Valle didn't shoot, but whoever was in the woods did. A chunk of bark jumped off the pine and sailed away.

Calder ducked and hid his head behind the trunk. Valle rolled over a couple more times and lost herself in the trees.

Calder didn't figure he'd say anything else to her. Valle had sense enough not to shoot him, or he hoped she did, and that ambusher was likely to blow his head off if he stuck it out again. Calder sat where he was. It was up to Fargo to take care of things now.

Fargo wound his way through the firs and pine trees, circling around the position where the shot fired at Valle had come from.

It didn't take him long to get where he was going. From his new vantage point he could see two horses and a body lying on the ground with a hat covering its face.

He could also see an occasional glimpse of a cloth shirt in the bushes and thought he could sneak down and get the drop on whoever was hiding there without being heard, but once again that day a plan went wrong through no fault of the person who'd made it.

This time a squirrel caused the trouble. Just as Fargo was about to ease his way down to Hap's position, a gray squirrel on a limb not far above the Trailsman's head started chattering, maybe angered that Fargo had intruded into his territory or maybe just because he felt like it.

The reason didn't matter. A thrashing in the brush told Fargo that someone had heard, and sure enough the bushwhacker revealed himself. Fargo recognized him as Hap Bryson, in the heartbeat before Hap started shooting.

Fargo dodged behind a tree, drawing his Colt as he did so, and put his foot wrong. His ankle twisted and he fell, hitting his forehead on the rough bark. The heavy revolver fell from his hand.

Hap saw Fargo fall and ran toward him, pistol ready to fire the killing shot.

Fargo shook his head to clear it and felt around for the Colt. All his fingers found was a dry stick. He didn't think the stick was going to help him.

Hap stopped about ten feet away from Fargo and grinned.

"Thought you could sneak up on me," he said. "Well, you was wrong." He looked at Fargo more closely. "I'll be damned. You're the one shot Willie. You didn't know you were doin' me a favor when you did it, so I thank you for that. Now I'll do a favor for you."

He raised the pistol, still grinning over the barrel.

Fargo heard a shot, but he didn't feel a thing because it wasn't Hap who'd pulled the trigger.

The top of Hap's head blew off, and if Hap felt anything at all, he didn't feel it for long. His body collapsed and didn't even twitch.

Valle walked up and looked down at Hap's remains.

"He killed my cocks," she said. "He and his brother did. His brother's back there. He's dead, too."

She sounded dazed, and she had a blank look in her eyes. Fargo reckoned Valle had never shot anybody before, much less killed him.

"I didn't mean to kill him," Valle went on. "I was aiming for his arm."

"Hard to hit a skinny little target like an arm," Calder said, walking up behind her. "Don't worry none about killin' him. He'd've killed you if he could. Already tried it, come to think of it. I don't expect he's any great loss to the world." He glanced at Fargo. "You doing all right?"

Fargo touched his forehead with his fingers. He didn't feel any blood, but there was a goose egg rising already.

"I'll live," he allowed. "Thanks to Valle."

He put a hand on the tree trunk and stood up. He didn't feel dizzy, and his ankle didn't twinge.

"Looks like the Bryson boys won't be goin' on from here," Calder said. "What're we gonna do about 'em?"

"We might as well bury them," Fargo said. "It's going to be dark in a little while, and we won't be able to follow the trail."

"I don't have a shovel," Calder said. "Might be one strapped to a Bryson horse. I'll look."

"What about my mule?" Valle said.

The heavy Colt dangled from her right hand. Fargo took it and stuck it in his belt.

"We'll look around for it," he said, putting his arm around Valle's shoulders and turning her away from Hap's corpse.

Calder didn't find a shovel, but he found the money in the saddlebags.

"What you reckon we oughta do with it?" he asked.

"Take it with us," Fargo said. "And then take it back to the bank."

"Yeah, if we don't get killed along the way. What about the Bryson boys?"

Fargo didn't want to leave the bodies out in plain sight, so he and Calder pulled the Brysons farther from the trail and covered them with brush.

"Good enough for a pair o' polecats like them two," Calder said when the job was done. "They wouldn't've bothered to do that much for us if we was dead. Left us where we fell is what they'd've done."

They went back to join Valle, who'd gathered up some sticks and started a small fire.

"We've let the bank robbers get away," Valle said. "We should have kept going."

Fargo hunkered down beside her. "They won't be traveling at night. They might have gotten where they were going, but we'll catch up to them in the morning."

"Yeah," Calder said. "They can't be too far ahead of us. We weren't expectin' you to come along, though."

"They have my father. I had to do something, so when the fighting started in the barn, I left as soon as I could. I had to take care of the cocks first, but Mr. Torbett helped. I turned them over to him and rode to town. When I heard what had happened, I wanted to ride with the posse, but the marshal hadn't even gotten one together. If he does, they won't be leaving until tomorrow morning. So I followed you."

"Good thing for Fargo you did, too," Calder said. "That's a mighty good mule you got, but we got enough horses now for you to ride one of them if you want to."

Valle smiled and said she'd stick with the mule. Fargo didn't think it was a good idea for her to go with them the next day, but when he tried to talk her out of it, she told him flatly that she was going with him and Calder.

"Where you reckon the robbers are?" Calder asked, stirring the fire with a stick.

"Up in the mountains," Fargo said.

Sparks jumped in the fire, and Calder tossed in the stick to burn.

"That's a big chunk o' territory," he pointed out.

"We'll find them," Fargo said, hoping they wouldn't be too late for Valle's father when they did.

The next morning, Fargo was up before first light. He stirred up the fire and started some coffee. By the time it had boiled, Valle and Calder were awake and moving around. A little before the sun had started to sift through the tree branches they were on their way, Fargo in front, Calder just behind, and Valle in the rear, riding the mule and leading the Brysons' horses.

The outlaws' trail got harder to follow as they went higher. The trees were sparser, but the ground was rockier. Still, Fargo never faltered, trusting to his keen senses and his instincts, and after about three hours they were looking at the entrance to a cave from a safe distance away.

"I never heard of any cave bein' up in these mountains," Calder said. "They got 'em a mighty good hidin' place."

Fargo didn't disagree with him.

"You right sure that's where they are?" Calder said. "Maybe they went somewhere else."

"That's where they went," Fargo told him.

"How we gonna find out if they're still there?"

A wisp of smoke wafted from the cave entrance and rose up past the lichen-covered rock above it.

"See that smoke?" Fargo said.

Calder nodded.

"They're there," Fargo said. "Or some of them are."

Something moved in a small copse of trees, and Fargo pointed in that direction.

"Look over in those trees."

"Horses," Valle said.

"Guess Wolf's here, all right," Calder said. "What's the plan, Fargo? You got one, ain't you?"

"We need to get closer. Find out who we're dealing with."

"There was five of 'em left."

"Two were supposed to stay with Pa," Valle said. "That would make seven, not counting him."

"Well, Fargo?" Calder said.

There was no way to slip up unseen. The ground leading to the cave was too open. One person might get to the entrance, however, if the outlaws didn't suspect any harm. Fargo didn't like the idea, but he turned to Valle and asked if she wanted to risk it.

"Of course. If my father's in there, I want to help."

"You don't think they've already let him go?" Calder asked.

"He'd have met us on the trail if they had," Fargo said.

"You think Valle will be all right?"

Fargo nodded and told Valle to take off her hat. "They'll see who she is, and she'll be fine."

He wished he was as confident of that as he sounded.

"We could just wait," Calder suggested. "See if they let her pa go."

Fargo said something that he'd been thinking ever since they'd arrived at the cave.

"If they'd been planning to let him go, they would have done it already."

"Maybe they're waitin' 'til after breakfast."

"You really believe that?"

"Nope."

"How about you, Valle?"

"I don't know what to think," she said with the strain of continuous worry edging into her voice. "He should have been on the way home by now."

"Why don't you go check on him?" Fargo said. "We'll wait and see what happens."

"What're we gonna do if they give him up to her?"

"Go back and meet the posse, then bring them here."

"Likely ever'body'll be gone by that time."

"We'll follow them, then."

"I guess we ain't got too much of a choice," Calder said. "No use gettin' into a gunfight with 'em, them bein' holed up in that cave like they are. We'd never get 'em out of there 'til they starved."

Nobody said anything for a few seconds. Then Valle handed Fargo the reins of the two horses she'd been leading.

"I'll be back with Pa in a little while," she said.

Fargo wished he believed that.

Big Boy stood just inside the mouth of the cave, drinking coffee from a battered tin cup. When he looked out and saw someone headed in that direction, he dropped the cup and grabbed for his pistol.

Patrick Wilson sat nearby with his back against the cold stone wall of the cave. The coffee splattered on his leg.

"Watch out, Big Boy," Wilson said. "That coffee's hot. You could burn a man with it."

"Look out, yourself." Big Boy pointed outside the

cave. "Ain't that your daughter comin' along out there?"

Wilson jumped up and brushed at his pants where the coffee had hit them. He peered outside. Sure enough, Valle was riding toward them. He'd know that shining hair anywhere.

"That's her," Wilson said.

He turned his head to see if any of the others had overheard. Wolf Jensen had, and he was on his way to see for himself.

"Looks like that gal of yours got a little overanxious about me letting you go," Jensen said when he reached Wilson's side. "You should've left already. Now there's gonna be some trouble."

"No need for any trouble," Wilson said. "Just stick a pistol in my back and walk out with me. I'll get my horse and be on my way, with her none the wiser. She won't have to see anybody else."

Wilson wasn't sure he could trust Jensen not to stick the pistol in his back and pull the trigger and then kill Valle, too, but he didn't see any other way out of the situation. It wouldn't do for Valle to know he'd been a part of the bank robbery scheme and that he'd used her to help with it. He couldn't stand that.

"My share's already in my saddlebags," Wilson continued. "No need for anything bad to happen to me or Valle."

"We'll see about that," Jensen said. "There'd better not be anybody with her." He paused as if thinking things over. "All right, we'll try it. Get your stuff."

Wilson's gear was nearby. He tossed his saddlebags over his shoulder and picked up his saddle.

"You can leave your gun belt," Jensen said. "Just unbuckle it and let it fall."

Wilson did as he was told, using his free hand to work the buckle.

"You take him out, Big Boy," Jensen said.

Big Boy grinned. "I'd like that." His pistol was small

in his hand, and he rammed the barrel into Wilson's back. "Start walking. Not too fast, though, or I'll put a hole right through the middle of you."

With Big Boy right behind him, Wilson started to walk out of the cave. Jensen's voice stopped them.

"Hold it," Jensen said. "How the hell did your daughter know where we are, Wilson? Nobody in this whole territory knows about this cave. We're the only people who've ever been here."

There was one man who knew, but Jensen didn't think he'd mention that. He was surprised that he hadn't shown up as he'd said he would. Too bad for him, because Jensen wasn't going to leave any share for him in the cave. Big Boy would just steal it if he did.

Wilson didn't know the answer to Jensen's question, but he knew he'd better come up with something fast. He said, "She's a good tracker. She must've followed us from town."

"She better not be heading up a posse."

"Who's going to let a woman head up a posse? You don't see one, do you?"

Jensen looked carefully. "No. That doesn't mean there's not one. If you catch a hint of anything wrong, Big Boy, kill him. Kill the girl, too."

Big Boy's grin widened. "Can I have a little fun with her first?"

"I don't give a damn what you do with her," Jensen said. "Take him on out of here."

Wilson didn't like hearing what Jensen said, but he kept quiet. He and Big Boy left the cave, and as soon as they were outside, Wilson raised a hand and waved to Valle, who was seated on the mule about forty yards away.

Valle waved back. Wilson didn't see anybody else, and he prayed nobody was hiding anywhere. It would be too bad for him and Valle if there was.

"Get on over to the horses," Big Boy said.

Wilson headed for the trees. Valle snapped the reins

and spoke to the mule, which started in the same direction.

By the time Valle reached the horses, Wilson had slung his saddle on a bay and was tightening the cinch strap. Big Boy stood to one side, his pistol still aimed at Wilson.

"Howdy, Valle," Big Boy said, giving her an ugly smile.

Valle inclined her head to acknowledge him but didn't speak. Wilson got the cinch tightened and flipped down the saddle fender before turning to face his daughter.

"Glad to see you, Valle me girl," he said.

"I'm glad to see you, too," she said. "I was worried about you."

"No need to worry about him," Big Boy said. "We took real good care of him. Ain't that right, Wilson?"

"That's right." Wilson put a foot in the stirrup. "We'll be going now."

"No need to rush off," Big Boy said, walking toward Wilson's horse. "Tell Valle how good we treated you."

Wilson threw his leg over the saddle. "They treated me fine, just fine."

"We sure enough did," Big Boy said. He patted the saddlebags behind Wilson. "Real good. You oughta let Valle take a look at what's in here. Then she'd know just how good we were to you."

"You have a way of talking too much, Big Boy," Wilson said. His heart thudded hard in his chest as he wished that the bastard would just shut up and let them leave.

"That's what Wolf says, but I don't believe it. Don't try to ride off, Wilson. We got to show Valle your share of the loot."

"Loot?" Valle said, looking at her father. "What's he talking about?"

"Nothing a'tall, Valle me girl," Wilson said. He

leaned forward as low as he could. "Ride, Valle!" he shouted and put his spurs to the horse's side.

Wilson's mount leaped forward. Valle hesitated, then kicked the mule's flanks, but it was too late. Big Boy sprang to her side. He was faster than she would ever have guessed, and he wrapped the fingers of his huge left hand around her ankle and held it tightly while he put a couple of shots over Wilson's head.

"Looks like that sorry scudder got away," Big Boy said. "But I don't give a damn. I got something better." He leered at Valle. "I got you."

8

"Damn," Jensen said.

Big Boy was causing trouble again. It seemed that was about all he did lately. Well, it was too late to worry about that now. Wilson was already on the run, and Big Boy was heading back to the cave with Valle. He'd pulled her off the mule and wrapped her in his arms. She was kicking, scratching, and yelling, but without much effect. Big Boy didn't seem to mind any more than he'd have minded a pesky fly. Jensen knew he'd wanted Valle from the beginning, and now he was going to have her.

Jensen didn't care about that. Big Boy could do what he wanted. As for Jensen, he was getting out of here. He'd hung around too long already. If the girl could find the cave, it was possible the posse could find it, given enough time.

"I'm leaving now," he announced to the two men in the cave. "If you fellas want to go with me, you can come along. If you don't, you can go your own way, or you can stay around for a while. Won't matter to me."

The two men he addressed were Silas Burns and Gene Rand. They'd hooked up with Wolf Jensen a year or so earlier, back when he'd been planning his bank robberies, and they'd stuck with him ever since.

Burns was a small, compact man with curly hair and

a bristly mustache. He said he thought he'd take his chances with Jensen.

Rand was tall and rangy. He'd known Burns a lot longer than he'd known Jensen, so he was willing to trust his friend's judgment.

"I'll go with you two. What's that shooting about?"

"Big Boy," Jensen said as if that was explanation enough, and it probably was.

They'd just about gathered up their things when Big Boy came into the cave with Valle still struggling. She'd stopped yelling, though, and Big Boy took her over to where his saddle lay. Holding Valle encircled with one arm, he leaned down and undid the leather strings that held a lariat to his saddle. Then he started to tie Valle's hands behind her back. When that was done, he tied her feet together.

"You fellas leaving?" he said after he finished.

"Damn right we are," Burns said. "You're crazy, Big Boy. Anybody ever tell you that?"

Big Boy didn't seem to be bothered by the remark.

"All the time," he said with a chuckle. "Might even be the truth."

"Good luck to you," Jensen said, not really meaning it. "Most likely we won't be seeing you again."

"You never can tell," Big Boy said. "What about your partner?"

He was referring to the man who hadn't shown up. Jensen said, "You can give him your share if you see him."

"No chance of that," Big Boy said.

"Kill him, then," Jensen said. "We don't need him anymore."

"What's happenin'?" Calder said. "Is that Valle's daddy ridin' this way?"

"Must be," Fargo said. They'd watched Big Boy bring a man out of the cave and guessed it was Wilson. Fargo hadn't seen everything that happened in the

111

trees after that, but he'd seen enough to have a pretty good idea. "Big Boy's got Valle."

"You sure?"

"There they are," Fargo said, and he and Calder watched Big Boy carry the scuffling Valle into the cave.

"Well, that tears it," Calder said. "We got her daddy loose, and now she's been took. I'd rather have her than her daddy, by God."

Fargo felt the same way. He waited until Wilson was well clear of the trees and out of sight of the cave, then rode off to intercept him. He didn't have to go far, as Wilson had stopped his horse. He was looking back over his shoulder as if he wasn't quite sure what had happened.

"Mr. Wilson?" Fargo said when he was close enough to be heard.

Wilson turned quickly, reaching for a pistol that wasn't there.

"Take it easy," the Trailsman said. "I'm a friend. Fargo's the name."

Wilson looked wild-eyed. "What're you doing here, Fargo? And who's that with you?"

"Dodge Calder," the old-timer introduced himself as he rode up beside Fargo. "We both know Valle. We were helpin' her get you back from that bank-robbin' gang."

Wilson's shoulders slumped. "So that's how she found us. You brought her."

"Damned sorry we did, too," Calder said. "It's a sorry kind of an hombre who'd ride off and leave his daughter with skunks like that."

"I didn't intend for her to stay behind. I thought she'd ride away with me."

"She'll be lucky if she ever rides again after that big yahoo gets through with her," Calder said.

Wilson looked as if someone had gut shot him. Without saying a word, he whipped the horse's head around and headed back for the cave.

"Damnation," Calder said. "Now they'll kill the both of 'em."

Big Boy had no intention of killing Valle, not for a while at least. He had other ideas.

For a minute or so it seemed as if Burns and Rand might stick around and try for a turn of their own with her, but they both left with Jensen. They carried saddlebags heavy with the loot from all the robberies. Jensen wasn't worried about the load. He had a couple of extra horses to carry it, and from what Big Boy had told him, now he even had a mule.

Big Boy was glad the others were gone. He didn't like having anybody watch him, and he didn't like sharing. He also didn't like having his women tied up while he enjoyed them, but he knew if he let Valle loose, he'd have to knock her out to do anything. She wouldn't provide him with much entertainment in that case.

Not that he minded a little struggle, but he'd get that even if she was bound, and he could take his time with her. He licked his lips and smiled at Valle, who stared back at him with hate-filled eyes.

Big Boy's smile grew wider. This was going to be fun. He was sure of it.

Jensen, Rand, and Burns loaded the horses and were ready to leave when a man rode into the trees.

"I thought you weren't coming," Jensen said.

"I can see that," Ben Kinkade said. "I take it that you were leaving without me."

"You were supposed to get here earlier."

"I got lost in the dark. Had to take a roundabout way. Either that, or your directions weren't good."

Jensen ignored the gibe. "You're here now. You can go with us."

"I don't like it that you were leaving. I did my part, and I want my share."

"The hell you did your part. We had a mess of trouble at that bank."

Jensen didn't mention that when you came right down to it, Big Boy was the one who'd caused the trouble.

"What happened at the bank wasn't my fault," Kinkade said. "I'm not responsible for what my employees do. Now give me my money."

"You'll get it. Not here, though."

Jensen had hoped that Kinkade had been prevented from leaving town, maybe even gotten hurt in the fight he was supposed to start at the cockfight. The whole series of robberies had been Kinkade's idea from the start, but he hadn't wanted to dirty his hands with the actual stealing.

"The plan was that we'd divide it here," he said.

"The plan's changed," Jensen told him. "Something went wrong. You'll get your money, though."

"I'd better," Kinkade said.

He needed the money because of bad investments back east and gambling losses. He'd already borrowed heavily, and unofficially, from the deposits at his own bank, and the robbery would have the additional benefit of covering up his misappropriations. All he had to do was get the money from Jensen and get back to town without anyone being the wiser.

"Earl Langley's going to want his share, too."

"Where is he?"

"He trusts me to bring it to him."

Jensen thought that was probably a mistake on Earl's part. Kinkade was making a mistake, too.

"I never said I was giving Langley a share. You'll have to pay him out of your part if he gets anything."

"You can't pull that," Kinkade said. "I needed somebody to help stir things up, and I promised him a share."

"Right. *You* promised him. Not me."

Kinkade didn't say anything to that.

"What about the posse?" Jensen asked. "They'd better not be coming after you."

"They don't know a thing about me. They were supposed to leave at first light, but you don't need to worry about them. They'll never find this place. You told me where it was, and I damned near didn't." Kinkade indicated Rand and Burns. "What happened to the rest of your gang?"

"Do you really give a damn?"

"I guess not. More money for the rest of us if they're not here. Maybe I could take Earl's share out of theirs."

"No, you can't," Jensen said.

Kinkade was about to argue the point, but they heard a horse and rider approaching fast.

"Who's that?" he said.

Jensen didn't know, and he didn't plan to stick around to find out.

"Let's get out of here," he said.

Nobody argued with that, not even Kinkade. Jensen and his men mounted up, and they rode away from there, leading the extra horses.

Wilson pulled back on the reins, and before his horse had come to a full stop, he was off its back and running toward the cave entrance.

Fargo and Calder weren't far behind him. If their count was right, there were seven men in the cave. They were wrong, because they'd been misled all along and because they'd been out of sight of the cave when Jensen had left. But they didn't know that.

Fargo didn't think they had much of a chance against seven men, but he felt he had to do something about Valle, and he couldn't let Wilson try to save her alone.

Wilson ran into the opening in the side of the mountain, and Fargo jumped off the Ovaro and went after him, pistol in hand. When he arrived he saw Big Boy and Wilson already struggling. Wilson clung to the huge man's back with his arm locked around his neck and his legs around his waist. Big Boy hopped and twisted and flailed, but he couldn't shake Wilson off.

Valle was on the floor not far from Big Boy's stomping feet, scooting to keep away from them. She was the only one Fargo could see.

Fargo smelled smoke and bacon grease as he went into the cave. The remains of a fire were just inside the entrance. The Trailsman heard Big Boy grunting with the effort of his attempts to dislodge Wilson.

It was impossible to do, so Big Boy started to run backward. He was moving fast when he hit the wall. Or rather when Wilson hit the wall. Big Boy smashed him into an outcropping of the damp stone while running at full speed. Wilson screamed and dropped off Big Boy's back.

Big Boy must have seen Fargo or sensed that someone was there, because he didn't waste any time with Wilson. He turned and ran deeper into the dark cavern, where he disappeared almost at once.

Realizing that he could be seen outlined against the entrance, Fargo dropped to the floor just in time. A shot echoed off the stone walls and a bullet whipped through the air above Fargo's head. It hit a rock near the opening and ricocheted off another boulder.

"Damn it!" Calder said. He'd come into the cave right behind Fargo and dropped to the floor when he'd seen the Trailsman do so. "Why'd you let him get away, Fargo?"

Another bullet whined off the wall a couple of times before it stopped.

"Worse'n hornets, zingin' around like that," Calder said. "You gonna go after him?"

"Why?" Fargo said. "He's not going anywhere."

"He is if there's another way out of here. You ever think about that?"

Fargo had thought about it, but he didn't believe

there was another exit. He said, "You can go after him if you want to. I'm going to see about Wilson."

Still hog-tied, Valle was already scooting toward her father, who moaned softly where he lay.

Fargo crawled over to him before Valle got there.

"You all right, Wilson?" he said, knowing the answer before Wilson spoke.

"My back," Wilson said, his voice a husky whisper. "Broke, maybe."

Valle heard the last part. She looked at Fargo, who shrugged. There wasn't much he could do, except cut Valle loose. He reached down to his calf and slid the Arkansas toothpick from the sheath strapped to his leg. The big, razor-sharp knife sliced through the rope as if it were a sewing thread.

When she was free, Valle sat up and took her father's head in her hands to steady it.

"We can't move him," Fargo warned. "He'll have to stay here until we get help. Could be just a bad bruise, but we can't take a chance on that."

"Can't feel my legs," Wilson grated between clenched teeth.

That wasn't a good sign, but there was nothing Fargo could do about it now. And there were other problems to deal with. He looked around the cave. Calder did the same.

"Where's ever'body gone?" Calder said.

"We know where Big Boy is," Fargo said.

"Yeah. I meant the other six that was supposed to be here."

"I saw three of them," Valle said. "They left. I don't think there were any others."

"If I remember my 'rithmetic right," Calder said, "that's three short."

"There are . . . no others," Wilson said.

Fargo thought about what that might mean. He looked at Calder. Calder nodded. He'd figured it out, too.

So had Valle. "Pa . . ."

Fargo heard the sadness and hurt in her voice.

"I was with them, Valle me girl," Wilson said. "I needed the money."

"Speakin' of the money," Calder said, "what happened to it?"

"Jensen took it," Valle said. "Him and the other two men. You could catch up with them, Skye. They haven't been gone long. Stop them before they get away with it. If we give the money back . . ."

Fargo knew what she was thinking. Give the money back, and maybe Wilson wouldn't have to go to jail. Not that it mattered much now. In his condition, Wilson wasn't going much of anywhere.

"If we go after 'em, what about Big Boy?" Calder said. "That is, if he ain't got out through some back door."

"I don't think there's a back entrance," Fargo said again. He raised his voice. "I don't think we have to worry about Big Boy, anyway. The snakes will take care of him."

"Snakes?" Valle said.

"All these caves have them," Fargo said, keeping his voice loud enough for someone lurking in the dark to hear. "Not here in the front where the light gets in. They don't like the light. They're all back there where it's too dark for a man to see them."

Calder joined in. "I heard tell about a fella who got into a whole nest of 'em once. You can't hear 'em in the dark, the way they slither around so quiet-like. He had so many bites on him, he swole up big as an acorn-eatin' cow. Popped plumb out of his skin in a couple of places."

Fargo wondered if Big Boy heard what he and Calder were saying, or if he was even bothered by the thought of snakes slithering all around him. Some people weren't.

"It ain't so much that they hurt you when they bite," Calder went on. "Or so I've heard tell. Them fangs go in so slick you don't even feel 'em break the skin. But you sure feel it when the poison hits you."

Calder paused and looked at Fargo, who shrugged.

"If the snakes don't get him, there's the spiders," Calder said. "They're near about as bad as the snakes. Drop on a man from the ceilin', they do."

Fargo heard a boot scrape on rock somewhere in the darkness. Big Boy was getting twitchy. Fargo was even feeling a little twitchy himself. He gestured for Calder to continue.

"Spiders get in a fella's hair and even in his eyes. Cover up his face like whiskers. Poison him like a snake, 'cept he don't swell all over, just his head. Big as a pumpkin. Eyes get big as horse apples. That's before they pop out. Even if you don't die, you're blinded."

Fargo heard more scuffing and a kind of gagging noise from the depths of the cave. Apparently Big Boy *was* bothered, and he'd heard enough. He burst out of the darkness on the dead run, yelling and brushing at his face with his left hand.

His pistol was in his right hand, and he fired wildly without looking. The bullets whined off the walls and ceiling.

Fargo shot him twice in the chest.

Calder shot him once in the knee, then shot again and missed completely, the bullet whining off a wall and back into the darkness.

When the bullets hit him, Big Boy stopped as if he'd run into a wall. Then he fell forward, his left hand still slapping at his face to drive away the imaginary spiders. When he hit the floor, his fingernails scratched at the stone for a couple of seconds. After that his hand stopped moving.

"I got 'im," Calder said, holstering his pistol. "Hit

'im dead center. Hated to do it, but he'd've killed us as soon as looked at us. He was gonna do worse to Valle."

"His share of the money's still here," Valle said. She didn't sound the least regretful that Big Boy was dead. "Now you have to get the rest of it. You have to find Jensen and get it back."

Fargo didn't feel much of an obligation to get the rest of the money back. He'd tried to save Wilson, which he'd more or less promised Valle he'd do. Even though he'd been wrong about him, he felt a little sad at what had happened. He doubted that Wilson would ever walk again, even if he survived, which wasn't a certainty.

"I'll stay here with Pa," Valle said. "If the posse doesn't find us, you can come back for us. Big Boy must've had something to eat. We'll be all right."

"What about it, Fargo?" Calder said. "We gonna do it? Might be a good-sized reward in it."

Fargo didn't care about the reward. Money wasn't going to change the way he lived his life. But he didn't like the idea of somebody like Jensen getting away with the robberies. He didn't like the way the boss outlaw had tried to frame him, either.

On the other hand, he didn't like having been put in the position of allowing the robbery to take place, and that was Wilson's doing, in a way. When he weighed it all, however, the balance came down on Wilson's side, and getting the money back would be the right thing to do, anyway.

"All right," he said. "We'll go after them."

"And we'll get 'em, too," Calder added with a grin.

9

Jensen didn't know just when he decided he'd have to kill Ben Kinkade, but it couldn't have been too long after they rode away from the cave. The banker just wouldn't shut up about the money and about how they needed to stop and divide it now. He kept yammering about Earl Langley's share, too.

Jensen was damned sick and tired of hearing it.

"Right here," Kinkade insisted. "We can stop right here and make the split."

They were five miles from the hideout and a good ten miles from Jensen's destination near the Rogue River.

"I have to get back to Jacksonville as soon as I can," Kinkade said. "If I'm gone too long, people will wonder where I am, and I don't want that. Just give me my share, and Earl's, and let me get on back there."

His comments were met with silence. Maple leaves rustled overhead.

"Damn it, Jensen. I want my money. And Earl's. I want it now."

Jensen brushed his hand across his thick beard as he pretended to think things over.

"All right," he said with a nod. "I'll give it to you."

He climbed down from his horse and walked around to the side opposite Kinkade.

"It's right here in this saddlebag," he said, flipping

the bag open. The flap landed behind the saddle, and the horse's tail twitched.

At the same time he opened the bag with his left hand, Jensen pulled his pistol with his right. When he raised the pistol over the horse's back, Kinkade's eyes widened, and Jensen pulled the trigger.

Jensen's horse jumped forward, leaving Jensen exposed, but it didn't matter. Kinkade wasn't going to shoot back. The bullet had smashed through his neck.

Blood fountained from the wound as Kinkade toppled from his horse and landed heavily on the ground. His heart pumped a few more times, and blood soaked into the earth where he fell. Then the pumping stopped and Kinkade's agonized eyes glazed over.

Rand and Burns sat stolidly on their mounts as Jensen retied the saddlebag flap. When Jensen was back on his horse, Burns said, "What're you gonna do with him?"

"Leave him. We'll take his horse, though. And his pistol. Get that, Rand."

Burns looked at Rand. Rand shrugged and got off his horse. He took Kinkade's gun belt and hung it over his saddle horn. Burns took the reins of Kinkade's horse. He was already leading one mount. Another wouldn't matter.

They rode away and left Kinkade's body lying where it had fallen, in the middle of a pool of blood soaking slowly into the ground.

"How come you think there's four men?" Calder asked. "Wilson told us there was just three of 'em."

"Somebody joined them where they had their horses," Fargo said. "I saw the tracks."

"You didn't tell me."

"I didn't think it mattered."

"It does if we're outnumbered four to two 'stead of three to two. I like to know my chances."

Fargo didn't think one more would make any difference, not the way Calder shot.

"Who do you think the fourth one is?" Calder said.

Fargo said he didn't know, but if he'd been asked to make a bet, he'd have put his money on Earl Langley.

"He ought not to give us much trouble, then, the way that banker cleaned his plow for him."

"He might be better with a gun than he is with his fists," Fargo pointed out.

"Guess we'll find out, then," Calder said. "Sooner or later."

Fargo spotted the turkey vultures before Calder did. The big birds tipped from side to side on their wide-spread wings, riding the air currents as they circled above something along the trail Fargo and Calder had been following.

"I see 'em," Calder said when Fargo reined in the Ovaro and turned to him. "What d'you reckon they mean?"

"They mean something's dead. Or somebody."

"I know that. I mean, do you think whatever it is that's dead has somethin' to do with you and me?"

"Be a pretty big coincidence if it didn't."

"I was afraid that's what you'd say. Who you reckon's dead this time?"

"We'll find out soon enough," the Trailsman said. "Keep a close watch all around. We don't want to wind up being buzzard bait ourselves."

"Damn right we don't—least I don't. Sometimes I wonder 'bout you."

"Don't forget you're the one who got me into this."

"There you go again, sayin' I got you into this. I didn't do no such of a thing. You got yourself into it, and you know it. You could no more keep from helpin' out a pretty woman than I could resist a cold glass of beer if I had one in my hand right now, which I wish I did."

Fargo laughed. "You don't wish you had one near as much as that fella those buzzards are after."

"If it's a fella, he ain't wishin' anything. Anyway, might not be anybody. Might just be a dead skunk."

"There's more than one kind of skunk," Fargo said. "Considering it's right on the trail we've been following, I think one of the two-legged kind is waiting for us."

"Wouldn't surprise me any," Calder said. "We gonna go find out, or just sit here jawin' about it all day?"

"Let's go take a look," Fargo said.

When they arrived at the body, one of the buzzards was already there. He hadn't done anything yet, but he hopped a bit closer and took a peck at the dead man's bloody neck as Fargo and Calder rode up.

"I'll be damned for a dollar," the old-timer said when he saw who was lying there. "Ben Kinkade. What the hell's he doin' here?"

"He was in on it," Fargo said. Kinkade was the other possibility he'd considered when he'd noticed the extra rider. "Kinkade must have helped Wolf rob his own bank."

"Why'd he go and do a thing like that?"

"I'm sure he had what he thought was a good reason."

"Could be Earl was in on it, too," Calder suggested.

"Could be. Doesn't make much difference to Kinkade, though."

"Guess it don't."

"They took his horse with them," Fargo said. He pointed to the tracks. "Three men, three extra horses now."

"And a lot of money," Calder said. "You forget about the money?"

"I haven't forgotten. That must be why they killed Kinkade. Either he got greedy or they did."

"Wonder if they'll have any more fallin's-out before they get where they're goin'."

"It would help us if they did."

"Bad luck for one or two of them, good luck for us. We could use it."

"Don't ever count on luck," Fargo said.

"I'll try to remember that," Calder told him. "Seems like we're leavin' dead men all over the place. You think we oughta bury Kinkade?"

"If we had the time, I'd say we should. But we don't have time."

"We took care of Big Boy and the Brysons."

Back at the cave they'd dragged Big Boy outside and covered him with some rocks they'd found around the cave mouth. It hadn't taken long, but Fargo wished they hadn't taken the time to do it, if only because it had allowed Jensen to increase his lead over them.

"We can't spare any time for him," Fargo said.

"Just leave him for the buzzards?"

"That's what Wolf did. We can bury him on the way back, if we get back. Or if there's anything left of him."

"You're sure a cheerful fella, Fargo. Anybody ever tell you that before?"

"You're the first," Fargo said.

"Well, it's about time somebody did."

The high, steep banks along the Rogue River were covered by towering fir trees. The trail that Jensen rode along was close to the water and so narrow that it could hardly be called a trail. The water roared along scant inches away from the trail, foaming around the huge rocks in its path. If a horse put a foot wrong, it would surely slide into the water, taking its rider with it, and both would be carried off by the powerful current that churned the water into white-capped rapids. Or if one of the horses they were leading went in, there would be no recovering the money.

Jensen wasn't going to lose the money.

"It's getting too dark to go any farther," he said. The sun had already disappeared beyond the riverbank. Jensen blamed Kinkade for slowing them down, but he knew it was his own fault. It was a hard trip to where they were going, and he should have left the cave earlier. "We'll have to stop along here for the night."

"Stop where?" Burns asked, looking up at the darkening sky above the bank so close beside them. "There's no place to stop that I can see."

"Right around the next bend there's a wide place where a flat rock sticks out over the water. There's a cut in the bank that's got room enough for us and the horses. Has a little overhang that'll shelter us."

Jensen had scouted the place long ago, and he hoped his memory of it was accurate. He'd never intended to stop there, but he'd marked it in his mind as a place that would do in a pinch. Their real destination was a cabin a couple of miles farther along. It was about halfway up one of the hills, hidden in the trees, far off any real trail. He'd stocked it with enough provisions to get them through at least a couple of months. After that, when interest in the robberies had died down, they could leave for wherever they wanted to go—California, Texas, it didn't matter. If they were careful, no one would ever connect them with a few bank jobs in Oregon.

They moved slowly and carefully, the sound of the horseshoes on stone muffled by the noise of the rushing river. When they rounded the bend and found the wide place on the bank Jensen remembered, he almost sighed with relief. They'd be safe there for the night. And the next morning, they'd be where nobody would ever find them. This part of the plan had worked out just the way he'd thought it would.

"Man'd be crazy to try goin' along there," Calder said as he looked at the narrow path beside the river. "You sure they went that way?"

Fargo just looked at him.

" 'Course you're sure. You're the Trailsman, and if you say they did, they did." Calder paused. "Don't know as I want to try it, though."

"You don't have to, then. You can wait here."

"I never said I was gonna wait. Just said I didn't know as I wanted to try it."

"We can't try it now, anyway," Fargo said. "It's too late in the day. We might as well put our guns to our heads and pull the triggers as to follow that trail in the dark. We'll have to wait until morning."

"We might've lost 'em by then."

"Can't be helped if we do, but I don't think they're too far ahead of us. If they try to travel along there at night, we won't have to worry about them anymore. The river will take care of them for us."

"Sure would hate to lose that money like that."

Fargo shrugged. "It's not our money."

"Guess not. Where you want to make camp?"

Fargo looked around. "In those trees over there. We'll get an early start tomorrow, leave as soon as it's light enough for the horses to see the trail."

"I don't guess there's any other way to go."

"That's the way Wolf went. That's the way we have to go."

Calder nodded. "I was afraid you'd say that. Part of your cheerful nature."

"Glad I could make you happy," Fargo said.

Fargo awoke the next morning to the constant roar of the river. The sky was overcast. Heavy clouds obscured the sun and threatened rain, but Fargo didn't let the weather change anything. He rousted Calder out of his bedroll and told him to get ready to travel.

"You ain't even gonna fix any coffee?" Calder said after he yawned and stretched his joints.

"No time for that. We have to get going. You don't want Wolf to get away, do you?"

Calder looked at the river. "Don't much care anymore."

"That trail's not as narrow as it looks," Fargo lied.

"Sure it ain't. I kinda wish I had Valle's mule. Mule's a lot more sure-footed than a horse."

"Your horse will be fine. If Wolf could go that way, we can. Or do you think your horse is that much worse at walking a trail than his?"

"Don't you go talkin' about my horse like that. My horse is as good as that bank robber's nag any ol' day."

"That's what I think, too. Now get ready and let's get out of here."

Calder grumbled some more, but he was ready quickly and they started out. The footing was treacherous, but they took it slow and careful. Calder complained most of the way, but the rain held off, and they didn't meet with any real trouble. In a little less than two hours, they reached the place where Wolf had camped.

"We were mighty close to 'em," Calder said. "Hadn't been for them rapids, we'd have been able to hear 'em snorin'."

Fargo doubted it. The water was so loud that he hadn't even heard Calder's snores, and the old-timer hadn't been more than ten feet from him.

"They had 'em a better place than we did," Calder said.

"They've been here before, I think. Or one of them has. Wolf's not just running away. He knows where he's going."

"Wonder if he knows we're following him."

"If he did, he'd have ambushed us before now."

"So we're gonna surprise him."

"We're going to try," Fargo said. "There's a difference."

"I believe I mentioned a couple of times what a cheerful fella you were. Guess I won't say it again."

"Good," Fargo told him.

The river smoothed out about a mile or so farther along, and the trail widened. It was still too narrow for two horses to walk side by side, but it made riding one horse a more comfortable proposition, and they could travel a little faster. Thunder rumbled in the distance, and lightning flashed in the clouds.

"Gonna rain, sure as the world," Calder said.

"Now who's being cheerful?" Fargo asked.

"Just statin' a fact. You reckon Wolf's ever gonna stop? Or do you think he's headed for Canada?"

"No way of knowing," Fargo said. "If he's going to Canada, he'll never get there. We'll catch him before he does."

"I hope we catch him quick, then. I'm gettin' tired of this river."

"He's not far ahead," Fargo said. He pointed. "Fresh horse apples. We need to be quiet now."

Calder didn't say anything, and Fargo looked back at him.

Calder put a finger to his lips and nodded.

Fargo grinned.

An hour later, he saw where the horses had left the trail, headed up the bank into the trees. He reined in the Ovaro, and Calder stopped behind him. Fargo pointed up the bank.

"What you reckon's up there?" Calder whispered.

"Old trapper's cabin, maybe," Fargo said. "Or a miner's cabin. Maybe another cave. Or maybe nothing. Could be Wolf's just decided to find an easier trail to travel on."

Fargo didn't think that was the case, however. Wolf must have had a destination in mind when he started out, and he wouldn't have come along this way in the first place if he'd been planning to take an easier route later on.

"We gonna go up there?" Calder said.

"He's not going to come to us."

"Guess not. How we gonna do this?"

It was a good question. The bank wasn't as steep here as it had been by the rapids, and it would be easy to follow Wolf's trail, but they couldn't just go straight ahead, not if Wolf had gone to ground. They might surprise him, but they might not. He might be too wary for that. And if he was, he might have a surprise or two for them instead of the other way around.

"I'll go take a look and see what I can see," Fargo said. "If Wolf's up there, I'll come back for you, and then we'll figure out what to do next."

"You sayin' I make too much noise to go along with you—is that it?"

"I'm saying it's better for one of us to see what's up there than for both of us to go. If I don't make it back, you can get help."

"Ain't nobody gonna help me. No posse's gonna try that trail. We're on our own, and you know it."

"Remember, you're the one—"

"—who got us into this. You can keep saying it, but that don't make it true."

Fargo grinned. "I'll be back. You find somewhere to stay out of sight."

"You better let me know it's you when you come back, else I might have to kill you."

Fargo thought he'd be safe, but he said, "I'll give a whistle."

"You do that," Calder said.

Fargo dismounted and pulled his Henry rifle from the scabbard strapped to his saddle.

"I'll trust you to take care of my horse," he told Calder, and then he walked away.

The rain started before he was out of sight.

Jensen wasn't happy. It wasn't the cabin. Sure, it was run-down and dirty, and varmints had been after some of the supplies. But that wasn't what was bothering him. He'd known about the condition of the place, and he'd expected some small animals might get inside. Those were little problems and easy to fix.

What bothered him was something else, something he couldn't even explain, a feeling like a hunted animal might get when somebody was after him.

He told himself that it was just nervousness. After all, he had a lot of money with him, and he'd robbed four or five banks. There were bound to be people hunting him. A posse from Jacksonville, for sure. Maybe others, people hoping for a reward.

Even as he tried to convince himself that there was no danger, however, he became more certain that somebody was getting close to him.

He thought back and remembered the rider they'd heard coming hard back at the cave. He wished now he hadn't been in such a hurry to get away. If he'd stuck around and had a look, he would've known who it was.

Wilson coming back? Could be, but why? To see about his daughter? Made sense, but Wilson wouldn't have followed him all the way here. Big Boy would have made sure of that. Who else could it have been, though? Jensen didn't know, and that worried him.

"We got enough dust and dirt in this place to start a farm with," Rand said, breaking into Jensen's thoughts. "How long's it been since anybody lived here?"

"Haven't been any miners in this area for years," Jensen said. "Nobody ever found any gold here. I knew a fella once who told me about this place, and I had a look at it a while back. We won't be going anywhere for a while, so we got plenty of time to clean it up."

"I ain't much for cleaning up," Rand said.

He was so tall that his hat nearly brushed the ceiling, and he took it off, brushing at the cobwebs it had accumulated.

Burns sat down on a cot by the wall. Dust puffed

out of the thin covering, and he waved it away with a hand.

"I ain't much for cleaning up, either," he said, "but it looks like it's gotta be done."

"That's not all," Jensen said. "I got a feeling. Like somebody's out there. We need to keep a sharp eye out."

"Couldn't anybody follow us along that trail," Rand said. "I thought we weren't gonna make it ourselves."

"Doesn't matter what you thought. It won't hurt to be careful."

"He's right," Burns said. "We've come this far, and I don't want to lose the money now."

Money, Jensen thought. Could Earl Langley be the one on their trail, wanting his share? It didn't seem likely. Kinkade said he was going to take Langley's money to him. Who did that leave? Nobody came to mind.

Rain started to patter on the roof. Burns looked up and said, "How much you wanna bet it leaks?"

"Won't hurt you to get wet," Rand said. "Might do you some good. Not as much good as a bath, but some."

Wolf didn't even hear them. He was too preoccupied by his other worries.

"I'm going to go out and have a look around," he said. "You two can start cleaning this place up."

He went to the corner where he'd thrown his saddle and pulled his rifle from its scabbard. He hefted it in his hand, looked around the room, and left.

As soon as Jensen was out the door, Rand walked over to where Burns sat on the bed.

"You think he's just trying to get out of doing any work," Rand said, "or is he really worried?"

"He sure looked spooked to me," Burns said. He stood up. "Besides, he wouldn't go out in the rain just to get out of a little work. I think he's worried, all right."

"What about you?"

"I don't know. Maybe he's worried about nothing. Let's see if we can get started on cleaning this place up a little and worry about that instead of somebody that might be after us."

Outside, Jensen walked through the trees thinking about what to do next. If somebody was really out there, he was going to have to do something about it. He hefted the rifle again. He wasn't much of a shot with a rifle, but having it in his hand made him feel better.

It wasn't raining hard, just a thin drizzle. Jensen walked into the trees where the shadows were dark. He kept to the shadows and hid himself behind the trunks. When he found one that was big enough to conceal him and still give him a view back down the bank if he poked his head around it, he sat down.

The rain stopped almost as soon as he settled in, and the sound of the thunder faded off to the east, though the clouds still darkened the sky. Water dripped off the ends of the pine needles, but it was hardly noticeable. Jensen squirmed around and tried to get comfortable while he waited.

He didn't have to wait for long. He saw something move in the shadows along the side of the trail, and he was sure it was a man. Jensen was ordinarily calm, a man who had a plan for everything, but not for this. The plan had been disrupted, and he didn't know why or how. He just knew something had gone wrong, and instead of being calm and deliberate, he pulled the trigger of the rifle before he'd even thought about it. The heaviness of the air seemed to flatten the sound of the shot.

He jacked another cartridge into the chamber and fired again, though he didn't have a target and had no idea whether he had hit anything with his first bullet.

He paused and scanned the trees below. Nothing moved. Jensen stood up and ran for the cabin.

*   *   *

Fargo felt the bullet burn across his shoulder and fell to the ground, rolling into the brush. He'd been careless and he knew it. He should have known someone might be watching the trail, and even though he had kept to the side and in the trees, someone had spotted him.

He touched his fingers to his shoulder. The shirt, Wilson's, was torn, and his fingers felt the stickiness of blood, but the wound was no more than a scratch. He'd been lucky.

For several minutes he lay where he was, not moving. He strained his ears, but all he heard was the quiet drip of the water from the trees. He looked around for something to throw and saw a stick that he could reach. He took it and threw it as high and as far as he could. It hit a branch, shaking water loose before it fell.

Nothing happened. Whoever had shot him was either gone or too smart to waste a bullet on a stick. Fargo waited another minute, then got to his feet and started in the direction from which the shots had come. It didn't take him long to find the empty shell casings where they'd fallen. He could see the cabin through the trees. That had to be where Wolf had gone to ground, and now he knew that Fargo was on this trail.

Fargo hated it that he'd given Wolf a warning.

He hated it almost as much as the fact that he'd have to admit it to Calder.

10

Jensen came into the cabin on the run. Burns and Rand were gone. So were their saddles and saddle-bags.

Jensen grabbed his own saddle and took it in back of the cabin where the horses were crowded in a small corral. Burns and Rand were there, just about ready to go.

"We heard the shots," Rand said, pulling on a cinch strap. "We figured we'd take our share and leave."

"Go anytime you want to," Jensen said. He didn't care what they did. "I'm leaving, too."

"We didn't take any of your share," Burns said. "It's still in the cabin. We didn't take Kinkade's or Wilson's, either. What we have is enough for us."

Jensen didn't answer. He went back into the cabin for the saddlebags.

"You reckon we oughta take one of the spare horses?" Burns said.

"Hell, no," Rand said. "Let's light a shuck out of here."

Burns nodded, and they did.

Jensen saw them ride past the open door of the cabin. It didn't matter to him that they were gone or where they were going. His only concern was that his plan was ruined. He'd thought he'd be safe in the cabin, but he'd been wrong. Even if he'd killed the man he'd shot at, there'd be more coming. Hell, there must have been more than one after him, anyway. They'd be at the cabin soon, and he wanted to get away from there.

He didn't know where he'd go, and the thought left him hollow. He'd never been without a plan, and now he didn't have one. But he'd think of something. He always did.

"You let somebody shoot you and get away?" Calder said, looking at Fargo's shoulder. "I thought you were gonna be quiet. I thought you left me here because I was too noisy, and now you come back all shot up."

"It's nothing," Fargo said. He was wet, and his shoulder stung. He didn't feel like putting up with Calder's jabber. "We're going to have to get up there before Wolf gets away. Come on."

He swung himself aboard the Ovaro. Calder didn't move.

"Well?" Fargo said.

"You ain't gonna put somethin' on that arm?"

"You have anything?"

"Got some whiskey. Not much, and I been savin' it. But I might as well use a little on you. No use goin' around with an open wound."

It wasn't much of a wound, but Fargo knew Calder was right. He got down and let his friend pour some of the whiskey on the wound. It burned like fire, so it must have been doing some good. Calder put the whiskey away and put a piece of cloth over the shoulder, tying it under Fargo's arm.

"That's part of a clean shirt," he said. "My last one, in fact. Oughta hold you."

Fargo thanked him and climbed back on his horse. "Let's move."

"I'm right behind you," Calder said.

They went up the bank as fast as they could, but of course no one was at the cabin when they arrived. It took Fargo only a minute or so to find two different trails leading away from the corral where a couple of horses remained.

"Two men went east," he said. "One went west. He's leading two horses."

"Yeah. Didn't want all of 'em, I guess. You want to split up?"

Fargo didn't think that would be a good idea. He wasn't sure what might happen to Calder if he tangled with Wolf or with the other two on his own.

"We'll go after the two men who left together first. After we get them, we'll come back and track Wolf."

"You're sure it's him?"

"Bound to be. We'll get him, though."

"Not like you to be so certain about things."

"Well, I could be wrong."

"That's more like it," Calder said. "What're we waitin' for?"

They caught up with Rand and Burns in less than a half hour. The bank robbers had headed back toward the river to find the broad trail they'd left the previous night when they turned toward the cabin, but they'd been slowed by the fact that they weren't familiar with the territory. They'd just made it to the river when they saw Fargo and Calder behind them. They took cover among the cedars, oaks, and chinquapin that lined the bank and started shooting.

Fargo and Calder sought cover in the larger trees. Fargo unsheathed his Henry rifle as he dismounted.

"We gotta flush 'em out of there," Calder said as a bullet severed a small limb above him and sent pine needles flying. "The longer they stay in that brush, the farther away Wolf is gettin'."

"I might be able to get closer," Fargo said. He handed the rifle to Calder. "You keep them busy."

"Busy? With this here Henry, I can't miss. If one of 'em so much as shows an eye in one of them bushes, I'll shoot it out."

"Do it if you can," Fargo said. "Now."

Calder fired the Henry, and Fargo ran to the next tree as the answering shots went toward Calder's position.

Fargo didn't think Calder had hit anybody, but it didn't matter. At Calder's next shot, Fargo moved again, and this time he caught sight of color not natural to the brush, a man's shirt, most likely. He chanced a shot with his Colt.

A man yelled, and there was some thrashing in the brush. Fargo moved closer and fired again in the same general direction. No one yelled this time, but Fargo heard something moving around in the brush.

A tall man on horseback burst out of the bushes, leaning as far forward and as close to the horse's neck as he could.

He didn't get close enough. Fargo shot him in the side, and he pitched off the horse and back into the cedars and oaks. The horse kept right on going.

Fargo was cautious in approaching the river shore. He wasn't sure that both men were dead, though the tall one most likely was.

He checked that one first. He lay under a low-growing cedar, not moving. Fargo's bullet had struck him under the left arm and gone straight into his heart.

A limb rustled nearby, and Fargo turned. Through the thick limbs he saw a short man trying to get on his horse. He was having trouble because one arm hung useless at his side.

"Just stand still," Fargo said. "You're not going anywhere."

"The hell I'm not," the man said.

He ducked under the horse and pulled his saddlebags off when he reached the other side. Fargo shot at his legs, but the man zigged out of the way.

The river flowed fast at that point, but there weren't any rapids. Fargo didn't know how deep it was, but he figured it was too deep to wade and too cold and swift to swim.

The bank robber either didn't believe that or didn't care. Or maybe he just didn't see any other way out. He jumped into the water and started to float away on his back, but the saddlebags dragged him down.

Fargo reached the shore just as the man's head popped out of the water.

"Let go of the saddlebags," Fargo called.

The man spluttered and wrapped both arms around the leather bags. Then he went under again. His head showed up again, but this time the man was struggling, waving his arms as the current carried him along. The saddlebags had disappeared, not that letting them go was of any use. The outlaw was pulled under by the current again, and Fargo didn't see him after that, though he watched the water until Calder came down to join him.

"Reckon we could find those saddlebags?" Calder said after Fargo told him what had happened.

"How good a swimmer are you?"

"Not much better'n that fella was."

"Then we can't find them, because I'm not going in that river," Fargo said.

Calder shook his head. "Lot of money in those bags, I bet."

"Not worth your life, though, is it?"

"Nope. What about that fella you killed? His saddlebags must still be on his horse. Be easier to catch the horse than to go for a swim, I reckon. But we got us another dead man to deal with now."

"We'll just have to leave him," Fargo said. "We need to get after Jensen."

"People could track us by all the bodies we've left behind us," Calder said. "If they was of a mind to."

Fargo didn't want to think about that.

"Let's catch that horse," he said.

It didn't take them long. The horse hadn't gone far, and it wasn't spooked. Now they had two more horses to go with those in the corral.

"We could take him with us," Calder said, toeing Rand's body. "Bury him back at the cave."

"We have to get Jensen first," Fargo reminded him.

"So we're gonna just leave the horses here?"

They could leave the horses in the corral, or they could turn them loose to make it on their own. Neither idea appealed to Fargo. Leading them just wasn't a choice.

"We could come back for 'em," Calder said. "Or send somebody."

"Who'd come for four horses?"

"If you left the money, the sheriff'd send somebody."

Fargo thought that might be right, and he didn't think anybody would stumble across the cabin by accident.

"Plenty of hay in that lean-to by the corral," Calder said. "They'd be all right for a few days."

"All right," Fargo said. "We'll leave the horses and the money. If we don't catch up with Jensen, we can come back ourselves."

"Let's go put these two up, then," Calder said. "Jensen's gonna be in Texas before we catch him."

"He won't get that far," Fargo said.

It hadn't taken Jensen long to come up with a plan, and it didn't involve going to Texas.

He was going back to the cave. If Big Boy was still there, the two of them could stand off an army. If the woman was alive, they'd even have a hostage.

Jensen thought again about the rider he'd heard before they'd left.

Wilson? He could handle Wilson. For that matter, Big Boy would have handled him already.

Earl Langley? He might have followed Kinkade, but Jensen didn't think it was likely.

Was the rider the same man who'd found him at the cabin? That was all right then. He was dead, or hurt.

And who were those two bastards in Jacksonville who'd started shooting at him and his men? Did they have anything to do with this?

It didn't matter, though, in the long run. The cave was his best bet. Maybe nobody would find him if he went back there.

It would be a hard day's ride, but Jensen was confident he could make it. He didn't want to get there after dark, however. If he was delayed, he'd have to wait until morning. He didn't think he'd be delayed. As soon as he'd fired the first shot from his rifle, he'd lost the feeling of being followed.

Things were looking up.

"He's headed back the way we came," Fargo said with a surprised shake of his head as they wound down the bank toward the river. "We're going to come out just about where they camped last night."

"Hell," Calder said. "That means we're gonna have to travel that damn narrow trail again. I'd just as soon not have to do that."

"Ought to be easier this time."

"Maybe for you. I'm an old man. I ought not to have to do things like that ever' day."

"You won't have to come back. Unless the sheriff sends you after the money and the horses."

"Don't have to worry about that. He'll send somebody he knows. You think Wolf's headed back to that cave?"

The thought had occurred to Fargo already, and he believed that was exactly where Jensen was going, like a wounded animal heading back to its burrow.

"Could be," he said.

"Wilson's not gonna be any help to Valle if Wolf shows up there. More like a hindrance."

"We'll just have to try to get there before Wolf does anything."

"Reckon we can do that?"

"We can try," Fargo said.

Wilson and Valle hadn't had an easy time of it. The cave was cold and damp, and the stone floor was hard. Making sure her father didn't move kept Valle awake much of the night.

His condition was the same in the morning.

"I think my back is broken for sure, Valle me girl," he said, his jaw still clamped tight against the pain. "I hate to believe it because I'll become a burden to you for life."

Valle shook her head. "Don't say that. You could never be a burden."

"And what about Pete Folsom? Would he want his wife to be taking care of a cripple?"

"I'm not married to him yet. If he doesn't want you and me together, I never will be."

"Now don't be talking like that, Valle me girl. He's a fine young man, and he'll be good for you."

"For you, too, or he can forget about me."

Wilson smiled, and they spent the day talking about happier times. Valle told him about the cocks and about how they'd fared in the fights.

"You'd have been proud to see them," Valle said. "They were strong from the first, and they never backed down."

When she told him that the Brysons had killed several of the cocks, he scowled and said, "I knew those two spalpeens were no good from the start." He paused. "I guess I'm no good either, else I wouldn't be here in a cave with a busted back. I'm sorry I ever gave in to the temptation. But I'll make it up to you, Valle. I promise."

He didn't add, *If I'm not a cripple or in prison.* He didn't have to. They were both thinking it.

That afternoon when Fargo hadn't returned, Valle began to worry about him. She went outside the cave and looked around, hoping she might see him riding up.

Instead, she saw Wolf Jensen. He was still some distance away, but there was no doubt about who it was.

She went back into the cave and said, "Wolf Jensen is coming."

"Give me my pistol," Wilson said. "And help me sit up."

Valle gave him the pistol. "You can't sit up. It might kill you."

"Pull me up and brace me against the wall, and don't be talking back to your old father."

"Jensen will kill you."

"Or maybe I'll be the one doing the killing. Don't you be worrying about me."

It wasn't easy, but Valle got her father up. He gritted his teeth and groaned.

When he was in position, he said, "Now, you take Big Boy's pistol and get out of here."

"I can't leave you, and Wolf's outside. He'll be here any minute."

"Don't argue with me, Valle me girl. If Wolf kills me, it's no great loss, but if he kills you, it's the end of the world. Take the pistol and go deeper in the cave. 'Tisn't really full of serpents and spiders like Fargo and Calder said."

Valle found Big Boy's gun belt where Fargo had left it. She pulled the pistol from the holster and went back to Wilson.

"There's no more time for talking," he said. "Go and be quiet. Wolf will never know you're there."

"But . . ."

"No talking. Go."

Valle had always obeyed her father, and the habit was hard to break.

"I'll go," she said, "but if he kills you, he's going to have to kill me, too."

"You were always impetuous, Valle me girl, but don't talk like that. And go!"

She went, darting back into the thick shadows just before Jensen came to the opening and shouted Big Boy's name.

"He's not here," Wilson said. "I took care of him. Show your face in here, Jensen, and I'll take care of you as well."

Jensen didn't answer.

"Thinking it over, are you?" Wilson said. "Well, I don't blame you. A man that's better than Big Boy is bound to be better than you, wouldn't you say?"

Wilson didn't fool himself. He knew that Jensen was just thinking over his choices. Sooner or later he was going to enter the cave.

"How's your girl?" Jensen called. "Big Boy have his way with her? Did you get here in time to see it?"

Wilson shifted slightly trying to ease the pain in his back. From his place against the wall he had a good view of the entrance to the cave, and he knew that Jensen stood just outside it.

"You can't rile me like that, Jensen. Valle got clean away, and she's probably leading a posse from Jacksonville here right now. If I was you, I'd be leaving as quick as I could."

Wilson heard movement outside. He knew that Jensen wasn't leaving. Probably he was trying to get to a place where he could see inside without being seen. There wasn't one, though; or Wilson didn't think there was.

"It'll be dark soon," Jensen said. "You won't be able to see me when I come in, Wilson."

It wasn't that late. Wilson could see light outside. He said, "And you won't be able to see me. Might be interesting for both of us."

Wilson knew even as he spoke that Jensen would be coming in any second. He couldn't afford to wait until it got dark. That would be an hour or more. Wilson aimed his pistol at the entrance and tried to hold it steady.

Jensen came in crouched so low that Wilson's first shot went right over him. Jensen dodged to the side, and Wilson's second shot missed as well.

Jensen didn't miss. He shot Wilson twice in the chest.

Wilson didn't make a sound, but the pistol dropped from his hand and clanked on the stone floor.

A bullet sang past Jensen's head, and he fell flat, scraping his face on the rock.

Tears wet Valle's face as she strained her eyes to see where Jensen had fallen. She knew she should have stayed quiet and not risked a shot. Her father had tried to save her from Jensen, and now she'd let him know she was there.

Maybe she'd killed him or wounded him, but she couldn't risk leaving her hiding place behind a large outcrop of stone to make sure. She'd have to stay where she was and hope he gave himself away. She wiped the tears away with her left hand and waited.

Jensen raised his head. He'd seen the muzzle flash and knew about where the shot had come from. It had to be Valle that was back there. He eased his gun into position and fired in her general direction.

When the answering shot came, he fired right at the flash. There was a whine when the bullet hit rock, but Jensen was also rewarded with a scream.

He didn't get up right away, however. He waited to see if there would be another bullet coming at him.

Nothing happened, and Jensen eased himself into a

crouch. Still nothing. He stood up and started toward the back of the cave.

Fargo and Calder were close enough to see Jensen's horse outside the cave when they heard the muffled shots.

"Looks like Jensen's here, all right," Calder said. "What're we gonna do about it?"

"Go get him," Fargo said.

"If he don't get us first. Can't just go bargin' in there."

Fargo didn't see any other way to go about it, and said as much.

"We can wait for him to come out," Calder said.

"What makes you think he'll do that?"

"Gotta come out sometime."

"Valle and her father are in there. What about them?"

"The old man's done for," Calder said. "You know that. That back of his ain't gonna get no better."

"And Valle?"

"Well," Calder said as he scratched at his whiskers, "I reckon we oughta do something about that if we can."

"That's what I said." Fargo swung down from the Ovaro. "I'm going to do it right now."

"I'll be right behind you, then."

"Stay out of sight. Don't come in the cave unless I call you."

"What if you can't call me?"

"Ride back to Jacksonville and get a posse."

"Be too late then."

"Maybe not to get Jensen. And don't forget that money at the cabin."

"I ain't forgettin'. Won't need to worry, though. You can handle Jensen."

They heard a scream from the cave. Fargo ran in without another word to Calder.

Inside the cave the light was dim, but Fargo could see Wilson propped against the wall, dead from the look of him. From the back of the cave came the sound of a struggle, and Valle screamed again.

Fargo saw two figures locked together in the dark, but he couldn't risk a shot. He ran toward them.

As he reached them, he saw that Valle was one of them. She had her back to him. He saw Wolf's bearded face over her shoulder.

Wolf saw him as well. He shoved Valle hard, sending her tumbling backward right at Fargo. Fargo opened his arms to catch her, and Jensen disappeared deeper into the cave.

Fargo felt blood on Valle's arm. He let her down gently and said, "Are you all right?"

"It's Wolf," Valle said. "He killed my pa, and he shot me."

Valle's shirt was torn, and Fargo looked at the wound. As best he could tell in the poor light, she hadn't been struck by a bullet. It was more likely that a fragment of rock had cut her arm.

"You'll be all right," Fargo said. "Dodge is waiting outside. You go wait with him. Let him know it's you before you go out, so he won't shoot you. Not that there's much danger of that."

Valle managed a weak grin. "I'll be careful," she said.

Fargo helped her up and started her on her way.

Then he went after Wolf.

11

Wolf had disappeared into the deep darkness at the back of the cave. Fargo figured that he'd done a little exploring while staying there, which meant that he might know his way around even in the dark. He'd know where the tunnels branched. He'd know where the hiding places were. He could be any-where.

Fargo stopped just at the edge of the darkness, be-hind a rock. He had a feeling it would do no good to try the snakes and spiders trick on Wolf. He wasn't likely to fall for it, and Fargo didn't want to reveal his position.

He heard Valle call out somewhere behind him, and Calder answered. He was glad that she was safe.

He thought things over for a minute and didn't come up with any good answer to how he was going to get to Wolf. He was about to go back outside when he heard a scrape behind him. He looked around to see Calder working carefully along the cave wall toward him.

"Just like Big Boy," Calder whispered when he was beside Fargo. "We gonna starve him out?"

"You're the one who told me there was a back way into this place," Fargo said.

"Yeah, and you said you didn't think so. We have

the girl and the money. We can just leave Wolf here and go."

For an instant Fargo was tempted, but only for a second. It went against the grain to let Wolf get away with everything he'd done, including killing Wilson. Fargo couldn't let that go.

Then he thought of something else. Maybe they could spook Jensen out of there, after all. Not the same way they got Big Boy out, but close.

"Did you bring that blasting powder from the cabin?" he said in a loud voice, hoping that Calder would catch on.

Calder didn't answer for a second. Then his face brightened. He said, "Sure as hell did. I knew it'd come in handy. Glad that old fossicker left it there for somebody else to find."

Fargo hoped that Wolf hadn't explored the cabin and would believe the story.

"Be a nice way to bury Wilson, too," Calder went on. "Just blow down the side of the mountain and leave him in here with Wolf. Wonder how long Wolf'll last."

"We'll take out the supplies," Fargo said. "If he survives long, he'll have to eat Wilson."

"Reckon a fella'd eat anything to stay alive. Well, you get the supplies out, and I'll get the blastin' powder. That big rock right up over the top of the openin' will probably be just right to block the whole thing."

Calder made plenty of noise as he left, being sure to keep himself from being silhouetted in the entrance. The sun was going down, and the light was bad, so he didn't have much to worry about.

Fargo set about gathering up the supplies, banging around so Wolf would be sure to hear him.

He took a load outside, where Calder was explaining the plan to Valle. She had torn off a piece of cloth from her shirt and tied it around her wounded arm, staunching the flow of blood.

"You think he'll believe it?" she said.

"Maybe," Calder said. "If he don't, we might just leave him."

"What about Pa? You can't leave him, too."

"I'll bring him out after we get Wolf," Fargo said. "We'll bury him proper."

Valle nodded, and Fargo went back into the cave for the rest of the supplies. When he neared the entrance, he called out, "Be careful with that stuff, Dodge. You don't want to blow us up."

"I hear you," Calder yelled. "I'll cover that place so deep, nobody will ever find it again."

If there was indeed a back way out of the cave, Wolf would be there by now, Fargo thought. If there wasn't, he should be showing himself any time—unless he had more nerve than Fargo thought and was waiting for the explosion before he made his move.

Fargo thought he might tempt Wolf if he offered himself as a target. He unholstered his Colt and stepped into the cave.

"Last chance, Wolf," he said.

No answer came from the depths of the cave, but Fargo heard Wolf moving around.

"Light the fuse, Dodge," Fargo said.

"I'm doin' it."

Wolf stepped out from behind the rock where Fargo had concealed himself earlier. His right hand was behind his back.

"Hold it, Dodge," Fargo called out.

"Make up your mind," Calder yelled.

"Who the hell are you?" Wolf asked.

"Fargo's the name. Skye Fargo. The one you tried to frame."

"I should've killed you instead."

As soon as he spoke, Wolf moved his right hand to the front. He was holding his pistol, but Fargo was ready. Both men fired, Colt flame blooming in the shadows of the cave. Fargo heard the wind-rip of a bullet as it went past his ear, but it was Wolf who went down, shot through the body.

Fargo walked back to him and kicked the pistol away from his hand.

Wolf wasn't dead, not yet. He looked up at Fargo and gasped, "You sure . . . messed up my plans."

"That's the trouble with plans. Sometimes it's better not to have one. You got any for what happens next?"

"Never gave it . . . any thought," Wolf said.

"Most of us don't," Fargo said.

But he was talking to a dead man.

"You all right in there, Fargo?" Calder asked from the front of the cave.

"I'm fine. Wolf's not. He's dead."

"Good enough for him."

Fargo went outside. It was almost dark.

"We'll stay here for the night," he said. "Tomorrow we'll bury Valle's pa and take her home."

"Drag Wolf out here, then. Dead or not, I ain't spendin' the night with him."

The next day they returned to Jacksonville. The posse had given up the hunt for Wolf without ever getting near him, and the marshal was surprised to see him hanging across the saddle of one of the horses.

"Damnation," the lawman said. "You got him. I never thought I'd see you again. And you got the money, too?"

"Most of it," Fargo said.

He explained where the rest of it was, and the marshal said he'd send a man for it. Except for what was in the river. That was likely gone forever.

After the discussion of the money, Fargo explained Wolf's plan for framing him.

"You can bet I'll get the word out that you're not a

bank robber," the marshal said. "You can wear those buckskins of yours around here any time."

Fargo thanked him.

"You planning to stick around for a while?" the lawman asked.

Fargo said he didn't think so. "I'm not much for staying put in one place. But if I ever come back, I'll be wearing my own clothes."

They got back to the Wilson place a couple of days later. Pete Folsom was sitting on the porch. It was as if he'd been waiting for them. Maybe he had.

"You were gone an awful long time," he said.

He was looking right at Fargo, but it was Valle who answered.

"We ran into some trouble with bank robbers. Fargo and Dodge took care of them, though. I'll tell you all about it later, but right now I'm going to need some help around this place."

Folsom brightened. "I'd be glad to pitch in. That is, if your friends won't be helping you."

"We have to be getting on back to Ashland," Calder said. "I got a place of my own to look after."

"You can at least stay the night," Valle said. "You don't want to travel after dark."

"Well, all right. But we'll have to leave in the morning. Ain't that right, Fargo?"

"That's right," Fargo said.

Folsom brightened even more, though he didn't appear to like the idea that Fargo would be staying overnight.

"What about your pa?" he said to Valle.

"That's part of the story. You come back tomorrow, and I'll tell you the whole thing."

After Pete left, Calder saw to the horses. Valle and Fargo had time for a little talk.

"Pete's going to be good for this place," Valle said. "For me, too."

"I believe you're right," Fargo said.

Valle put a hand on his arm, and her touch was warm. "But Pete won't be here tonight, and Dodge snores mighty loud. He won't hear a thing that goes on."

Fargo grinned. He didn't care what Calder heard. Dodge wouldn't say anything. Much.

LOOKING FORWARD!
The following is the opening
section of the next novel in the exciting
Trailsman **series from Signet:**

THE TRAILSMAN #321
FLATHEAD FURY

Flathead Lake, 1861—where the poison of hate
destroyed innocent lives.

The rider came down out of the high country and
drew rein on the crest of a low hill. Below stretched
a long, broad valley. Mission Valley, some called it.
Beyond, to the north, gleamed Flathead Lake, the
largest body of water between the Mississippi River
and the Pacific Ocean.

The rider's handsome face was burned brown by
the relentless sun. He was tall in height and broad of
shoulder, and sat his saddle as someone long accustomed to being on horseback. In addition to buckskins, he wore a white hat turned brown with dust,
and a red bandanna. On his hip was a well-used Colt.
In the scabbard on his saddle nestled a Henry rifle.

The splendid stallion he rode was often referred to

as a pinto. A closer look revealed that the markings were different; the dark spots were smaller, and there were more of them. To those who knew horses, his was more properly called an Ovaro or Overo. But pinto would do.

The heat of the summer's day had brought sweat to the rider and his mount. The man removed his hat, swiped at his perspiring face with a sleeve, then jammed his hat back on and pulled the brim low. He was about to gig the Ovaro down the slope when movement drew his attention to a procession moving out of the hills.

The rider's eyes, which were the same vivid blue as the lake miles away, narrowed. Four men on horseback were strung out in single file. Trailing them were three shuffling figures in dresses, and unless the rider's eyes were playing tricks on him, the three women had their arms bound behind their backs and were linked one to the other by rope looped around their necks.

"It is worth a look-see," the man said to the Ovaro, and tapped his spurs. When he was still a ways off, one of the four men spotted him, and shouted and pointed. The party promptly halted. Two of the men moved their mounts to either side of the women.

The stockiest of the bunch came out and waited with the butt of his rifle on his leg and his finger on the trigger. He wore seedy clothes more common on the riverfront than in the mountains. On his left hip was a bowie. "That will be far enough, mister!" he called out when the tall rider had but ten yards to cover.

"What do you want?"

The tall man drew rein and leaned on his saddle horn. "Nothing in particular," he answered. "You are the first people I have come across in over a week."

The stocky riverman's dark eyes raked the other

from dusty hat to dusty boots. "Mind if I ask your handle?"

"Skye Fargo."

"I am called Kutler." The man paused. "Haven't I heard of you somewhere? Something about a shooting match you won? Or was it that you scout for the army?"

"Both," Fargo said. He noticed that the other three men had their hands near their revolvers.

"What are you doing in this neck of the woods? Army work?" Kutler asked with more than a hint of suspicion.

Fargo shook his head. "I have time to myself and wanted to get away by my lonesome for a while," he lied. He gazed to the north. "The last time I was through this area, the only settlement had a handful of cabins and a lean-to and called itself Polson."

"Polson is still there, but near a hundred people call it home these days," Kutler unwittingly confirmed the intelligence passed on to Fargo by the army. "By the end of next year that number will be a thousand."

"Did you just say a thousand?" Fargo grinned. "Do you have a flask hid somewhere?"

Kutler chuckled. "I do sound drunk, don't I? But I am as sober as can be. Not by choice, mind you. The man I work for has his rules. He is the one predicting there will be that many."

"He is awful optimistic," Fargo said. It was true more and more people were flocking west each year, but Mission Valley and Flathead Lake, were so far north, it would be decades yet before the influx rivaled that of, say, Denver or Cheyenne.

"Big Mike Durn has reason to be. He has it all worked out. If he says there will be a thousand, I believe him."

"I have heard of him but I can't remember where,"

Fargo told his second lie. The colonel had told him about Durn.

"No doubt you have," Kutler said. "Big Mike got his start running keelboats on the Mississippi. He became famous when he was in a tavern brawl and killed three men with his bare fists. Self-defense, the jury said. It was in all the newspapers."

"So he is *that* Big Mike," Fargo said as if impressed.

"The one and only," Kutler said proudly. "The scourge of the Mississippi, they used to call him. But he had to leave the river and wound up here."

Fargo studied the women. Indian women, they were, and not one had seen twenty winters. All three wore finely crafted doeskin dresses and moccasins.

"That was six months ago," Kutler was saying. "Now Big Mike pretty much runs Polson as he pleases."

Indicating the women, Fargo asked, "How do they fit in?"

"Their fathers or husbands borrowed money from Big Mike and can't repay him, so these squaws have to work off the debt."

Fargo was about to ask how when the man behind Kutler gave a harsh bark of impatience.

"Damn it, Kutler, how much longer are you two going to jaw? I want to get back. Another day without whiskey and my insides will shrivel." He was a small man with a hooked beak of a nose, a scar on his pointed chin, and a perpetual scowl. Like Fargo, he wore buckskins. Cradled in his left arm was a Sharps. A revolver adorned his hip.

Kutler glanced sharply over his shoulder. "That will be enough out of you, Tork. Big Mike put me in charge. We will ride on when I say we ride on."

Tork looked at the two men who were on either side of the women and made a show of rolling his eyes.

Fargo saw Kutler's hand drift toward his revolver, but for whatever reason, Kutler let his hand drop and muttered something under his breath. "Good friends, are you?" Fargo remarked.

Kutler snorted. "Tork doesn't like me and I don't like him. But so long as we both work for Big Mike, nothing much will come of it."

"Why is that?"

"Because if one of us kills the other, Big Mike will kill whoever lives." Kutler lifted his reins. "If you are ever in Polson, look me up. I am usually at the Whiskey Mill."

Fargo had to ask before they rode off. "You say these women are to work off a debt? How do they do that, exactly?"

"How do you think?" Kutler rejoined, with a wink and a leer. "They would run off if they could but we do not give them the chance." He clucked to his horse. "If any of these squaws strike your fancy, they will be at the Whiskey Mill, too."

The women filed past with their heads bowed. Judging by the way they wore their hair and the styles of their dress, two were Flatheads and one was a Coeur d'Alene. The youngest Flathead was quite pretty, with nice lips and full cheeks and beautiful eyes that fixed on Fargo's as she went by in what he took to be mute appeal.

"Get along there!" snapped one of her guards.

Fargo sat and watched them until they were stick figures. "Hell," he said to the Ovaro. His gaze drifted to the range of mountains to the northwest. Several of the peaks were so high, they were mantled with snow all year long. If he wanted to be by his lonesome, that was the place to go.

Fargo reined toward the lake. He held to a walk. There was no hurry, and the Ovaro was tired. The image of the pretty Flathead seemed to float in the air before him. "Now I have even more reason," he said aloud.

Fargo was looking forward to a hot meal, a bottle of whiskey, and a card game. He must remember to keep his ears pricked. As his friend, Colonel Travis, had made plain the night before Fargo left the fort: "Your orders are to find out if the rumors are true. If they are, get word to me, and I will take whatever measures I deem necessary. Unfortunately, since this is largely a civilian matter, I must be careful how I proceed or the newspapers will be clamoring for my hide."

Fargo had said that he understood.

"I wouldn't ask this of you but there is no one else I trust half as much as I trust you," Colonel Travis remarked. "But be careful. Don't get involved if you can help it."

"I will try my best not to," Fargo had responded.

Now, with the sun well past its apex, Fargo reckoned he would reach Polson about twilight. He came on an isolated cabin, and shortly after, a second homestead.

They were not there the last time he was here, and each brought a frown of disapproval.

The West was growing too damn fast for his liking.

Fargo rounded a bend and suddenly had to rein up to avoid riding into an old man in shabby homespun who was staggering down the middle of the trail, a nearly empty whiskey bottle clutched in his bony hand. "Watch where you are going, old-timer."

The man stopped and swayed, peering up at Fargo through bloodshot eyes. Taking a swig, he testily demanded, "What are you trying to do? Ride me down?" He was so drunk he slurred every syllable.

"If you don't want to be trod on, you shouldn't hog the trail."

Sniffing in resentment, the old man put his spindly arms on his bony hips. He wore a Colt Navy in a scuffed holster but he made no attempt to draw it. "For your information, I am almost out of bug juice and I am on my way into Polson for more."

"I reckon you have had enough," Fargo mentioned.

"What makes you say that, you busybody?"

"You are going the wrong way."

The old man gave a start. "How's that?"

"Polson is to the north. You are walking south."

"The hell you say!" The oldster glanced about him in bewilderment, then cackled and exclaimed, "I'll be damned! Somehow or other I got turned around."

"I wonder how," Fargo said drily.

The old man smiled and held out a hand. His teeth, the few that were left, were yellow. "Thaddeus Thompson, sir. Thank you for pointing out my mistake."

Fargo bent down. It was like shaking hands with dry bones. "It will be dark soon. Maybe you should go home."

"And not get my refill?" Thaddeus took a step back in indignation. "How do you expect me to make it through the night? When I am sober the nightmares are worse."

"Why would a gent your age have nightmares?"

Thaddeus grew even more indignant. "What does my age have to do with anything, you ornery pup? I have nightmares for the same reason anyone does. Because things happened that seared my soul. Because in the dark of night, the dead haunt us."

"For a drunk you have a way with words," Fargo complimented him.

Sorrowfully hanging his head, Thaddeus said, "They blame me, so they come back to remind me."

"Who does?"

"My wife, Martha, and my brother, Simon. They were murdered and there was nothing I could do." Thaddeus upended the last of his whiskey into his mouth, then uttered a low sob.

"Someone killed them?"

"I swear, you do not have enough brains to grease a pan. Isn't that what I just said? But I don't have proof so there is not much I can do."

"I would like to hear about it," Fargo said.

"Go to hell. It hurts too much. It is bad enough Martha and Simon crawl out of their graves at night to point fingers at me." Wheeling, Thaddeus staggered in the direction of Polson, swinging the now empty bottle by its neck.

Fargo kneed the Ovaro and came up next to him. "How about if we ride double? You will reach the settlement a lot sooner."

"When I get there, I get there," Thaddeus declared. "I would not go at all if I did not need more gut-warmer."

"It is a long walk," Fargo tried again.

"I am no infant. Kindly take you and your horse elsewhere so I can suffer in silence."

"I am in no hurry."

The sun was poised on the rim of the world. Soon only a golden crown remained. Then that, too, was gone. The sky gradually darkened, giving birth to stars, which multiplied like rabbits.

Thaddeus Thompson had been plodding along mumbling to himself, but he abruptly jerked his head up and wagged a finger at Fargo. "I thought I told you to mosey on. I do not need your company."

"It isn't smart to be out alone at night," Fargo observed. "The Blackfeet have been acting up of late. And there are grizzlies hereabouts."

"Hell, the Blackfeet have held a grudge since Lewis and Clark. As for the silvertips, most stay up in the mountains these days. To come down here is an invite to be stuffed and mounted."

"So the answer is no?"

"If your head were any harder, you would have rock between your ears."

Fargo had taken all of the old man's barbs he was going to. "And you called me ornery, you old goat. Have it your way," he said, and applied his spurs. But no sooner did he do so than the undergrowth parted and onto the trail strode the lord of the Rockies, the very creature Fargo had been concerned about. "Son of a bitch!" he exclaimed, drawing rein.

Apparently Thaddeus had not noticed the newcomer because he asked, "What has you in a dither, sonny?"

Fargo did not have to answer. The grizzly did it for him by rearing onto its hind legs, tilting its head, and growling.

No other series packs this much heat!

THE TRAILSMAN